Ava's Wishes

Book One: Whispered Wishes Series

Karen Pokras

Grand Daisy Press

Grand Daisy Press
PO Box 30241
Elkins Park, PA 19027

Edited by Melissa Ringsted of There For You Editing
Cover by Najla Qamber Designs
Models: Courtney Boyett and Willis Totten
Model Photographer: Casey Boyett
Book Layout ©2013 BookDesignTemplates.com

Ava's Wishes/Karen Pokras. -- 1st ed.
ISBN 978-0-9962843-0-1

For more information, please visit
www.karenpokras.com

"Where there is great love, there are always wishes."

—Willa Cather

The Whispered Wishes Series

Ava's Wishes
Holly's Wishes
Tessa's Wishes
Woven Wishes
Merry Wishes: An E-book Novella

Ava took a step back and admired her sketch. *If you'd seen one naked body, you'd seen them all.* In the three and a half months since she'd been enrolled in the Figure Drawing class at Wolfenson College, she really had seen them all—tall, short, thin, fat, male, female. She was getting tired of drawing the human form and was ready to move on to something else ... anything else. The models were mainly other students looking to make some extra money. She couldn't blame them. She was tired of being broke herself, although you couldn't pay her enough to pose nude. It's not that she was ashamed of her body. She just thought that some things were meant to stay private.

Drawing live nudes had been awkward at first, especially when it was someone she knew, but after a while, they were just bodies—no different really than a bowl of fruit or a vase of flowers. Still, she preferred to remain on her side of the easel and counted the days until the class was over.

The men were the worst. Ava hated to be judgmental, but most of the guys were full of themselves. They were okay in the looks department, however she'd seen better. She'd have liked to tell them so, but figured that would get her kicked out of a class she needed in order to graduate. Luckily, this was the final model of the semester. His name was Mark, or maybe it was Matt. She couldn't really remember, nor did she care. The important thing was finishing this course—one of the many required for her dual art and business degrees. Her big dream was to open up an art gallery one day.

"Ava!" Ms. Senaca snapped, pulling her out of her thoughts. "A little less gawking, and a little more sketching, please."

Feeling the heat rising to her cheeks, she returned to her drawing. The snickering from the other students didn't help.

"As if," she mumbled to herself.

Matt or Mark, or whatever his name was, looked straight at her and winked. *Oh great.* Her eyes darted back to her paper. The end of class could not come fast enough.

"He likes you, you know," whispered the voice next to her.

Ava knew better than to take her eyes off of her sketch to answer Carly. She'd already gotten in enough trouble for one afternoon. "Gross," she whispered back.

"Are we looking at the same guy? He's by far the best looking model we've had all semester. It's about time we got someone good. Why do you think I took this class?"

"Um, to develop your craft?"

"I'd like to develop something with him," Carly teased, smiling at the naked guy.

Ms. Senaca deliberately coughed and looked pointedly at the girls. They quickly turned their attention back to their easels.

Ava first met Carly Cater during Introduction to Watercolors the year before. She had already set up her supplies when Carly came rushing in late, like a bull in a china shop, dropping her paper and paints everywhere. Once she collected herself, she chose the only open station, the one next to Ava. She made snide comments every five minutes, and even got Ava in trouble ... much like she was trying to do today. Yet, somehow, they'd become friends. Not best friends; those slots were reserved for her sisters, Holly and Tessa, but they were good friends nonetheless.

"Oh! He's looking back over here. Quick, take that scowl off your face and try to look sultry."

She glanced over at her friend. Carly stared right at him and ran her tongue over her lips, slowly, sensually, as if he were a piece of meat, and she hadn't had a thing to eat all day.

Shaking her head, Ava's eyes gradually moved to the model, afraid of what she was going to find. "Ugh," she growled in disgust. The guy was too busy staring at her to notice Carly's obscene actions.

When he finally turned his head away, a smug smile on his lips, Carly whispered, "You should totally go for it."

"Yeah, *not*. Who does he think he is? He's something else." She'd had more than her fill of his inflated ego.

"Well, I think he's perfect, and his face isn't bad either!" A louder than probably intended cackle escaped Carly's lips.

"Girls!" Ms. Senaca bellowed. "Perhaps you'd like to share with the class what you find so funny this afternoon?"

"Nothing, ma'am," Carly offered. "We were only commenting on this model's extraordinary physique. He's been a pleasure to have in class, and a great honor to sketch. We've learned so much about the human form just from observing him. In fact, Ava was just telling me that his body was something else."

"Carly!" For the second time, Ava could hear snickers and felt the heat rising to her cheeks. "Ms. Senaca, that's *not* what I said."

"Well, what exactly did you say?"

"I wasn't talking about his... I really didn't say anything about his... I'm just trying to finish up my sketch, ma'am."

"Please do and without comment, if possible, hmmm?"

"Yes, ma'am." She glared at Carly.

"Good. In fact, everyone needs to finish up their sketches today. It's our last day with this model, and class is almost over. Tomorrow, you will sign up for studio time to work on your final exam projects. I'll expect five of your best sketches from the semester in a portfolio handed in to me by Wednesday."

"Thanks a lot," Ava whispered.

"You'll thank me later." She smiled, but looked back at her easel, her expression serious, when Ms. Senaca cleared her throat and walked by.

2

Ava was furious and refused to say another word to Carly for the remainder of the class. Even if it was only ten minutes, it was an extremely self-satisfying ten minutes. She finished her sketch and packed up her supplies as soon as Ms. Senaca announced, "Time's up!"

Carly tried to apologize, but Ava just ignored her. She'd gone too far, and Ava wasn't ready to let it go. Not just yet, anyway. She was the first one out of the room, practically running, without so much as a good-bye to anyone.

Once outside, she found a bench in the courtyard and sat with her head in her hands. It was a cold

December afternoon on the east coast, but she didn't care. She needed a few minutes. She pulled out her phone. Tessa or Holly? Tessa was only sixteen and would probably find the entire situation hilarious. Ava was usually the one dishing out advice where her baby sister was concerned. In fact, as the eldest of the three, she was usually the one dishing out advice where both of her sisters were concerned. But she needed to talk to *someone.* At least Holly, only two years younger, would be able to relate. Ava began to text:

Hol, you around? Crud of a day. Need a friendly voice.

While she waited for a response, she tightened the scarf around her neck. Why couldn't she have picked a school in a warmer climate? She knew the answer to that question. Initially, she had wanted to be close to her family ... her sisters in particular. Back in high school, when it came time to choosing colleges, her sisters were as involved in the decision making process as anyone. Wolfenson was only a two hour drive from home, although she could count the number of times her sisters had actually visited her at school over the past four years on one hand. Tessa was still in high school and immersed in her own activities, and Holly was more than a hundred miles away—in the opposite direction—at the state university. Despite that, they spoke nearly every day. Thankfully, distance made no difference in their relationship.

As far as colleges went, Wolfenson was one of the finest for liberal arts. Tucked away in a beautiful New England town, bursting with magnificent stone buildings, it was originally an all-girls school until it opened its doors to men back in the 1930s. Its undergraduate population was modest at only twenty-four hundred students, but Ava preferred the more intimate setting to the massive—and crowded—university Holly had chosen.

"How humiliating," she whispered to herself, remembering the scene in class with a shudder.

She was grateful she'd never have to draw another live nude model. In fact, she never understood why Figure Drawing was a required course to begin with. She'd never wanted to be an artist, she wanted to be the person who displayed and sold the art *other* people created. Yet, for some reason, she'd chosen to be an art major. She supposed halfway through her senior year was too late for regrets. For the most part, she'd enjoyed her classes—she wasn't half bad either—and if she had to choose between art and business classes, she'd choose art classes any day ... hands down.

Ava knew her business degree was just as important, maybe even more so, if she wanted to run a gallery one day, but the classes were brutal. She'd barely passed most of them, and one in particular, Statistics 101, she wondered if she'd ever pass.

Finally, her phone buzzed:

In class, will call later. Love you to pieces xo - Hol

Tucking her phone back in her pocket, Ava shook her head. It figured Holly would be busy when she was having the worst day she could remember in forever. Slouching back against the bench, she pondered her situation. On the whole, she'd found college to be pretty much a waste of time. She learned much more from her weekly internship at the Main Street Gallery. Ava had worked there every Friday night and Saturday afternoon for the past six months, and clocked even more hours when there was a special event, like the *Images in Flight* exhibit opening soon. She'd already told her parents she'd be staying up at school an extra week to help out with that before heading home for winter break.

Seeing Carly come out of the building, she twisted her body to hide behind the branches from an overhanging tree. Ava was in no mood to deal with more of her antics. Luckily, Carly was deep in conversation with a girl Ava didn't recognize. *Her next victim*, she thought, ignoring the tiny voice reminding her that Carly was her friend.

Once the coast was clear, she looked at her watch, grabbed her backpack, and headed toward her next class.

"Hey, wait up!" a masculine voice called out behind her.

Out of the corner of her eye she could see the model walking toward her. Ugh. She'd forgotten about him. She picked up her pace hoping he'd give up and leave her alone. Between Ms. Senaca and Carly, it was no wonder the guy thought she had the hots for him. The last time one of the models from class asked her out, it didn't end well. She wasn't in the mood to give it another try, especially with finals week quickly approaching. Maybe he was talking to someone else.

"Hey! You from the class! Can you slow down a little?"

She was wrong. *Damn.* Reluctantly, she stopped walking, allowing him to catch up to her. Now that Mark/Matt was fully dressed, she noticed his face for the first time. Really noticed it—the green eyes and full lips, the way the stubble on his jaws reminded her of every sexy actor she'd ever swooned over. In class they only sketched the nudes from the neck down, to protect their privacy—what a joke. She could feel the heat rising to her face for the third time in one hour. He certainly was good looking, but she'd never admit it. Not to him at least. It was more than obvious he already knew it. His ego seemed to be as big as his ... nope, she wasn't even going there.

"I'm going to be late," she said. "And I wasn't gawking, either. If you must know, I was thinking about something not at all related to you, or ... this."

Ava motioned her arm up and down his body as if he was some sort of prize in a game show.

"O ... kay," he replied, his dark brows arching. "Actually, I was only trying to catch up with you because you left your portfolio behind. You ran out so quickly, you forgot it. Ms. Senaca spotted you in the courtyard and asked if I could run it out. Everyone else was gone by the time she noticed, but I was still in the studio getting dressed. You know, trying to cover up all ... this." He motioned his arm in the same fashion, smirking. "Anyway, she thought you might need it with finals coming up. So, here you go. See you around."

"Oh." Ava was too shocked to get the words *thank you* out of her mouth before whatever his name was turned around and walked away.

3

"Pay attention, will you?"

The silence in the study room Ava reserved at the student center was broken by the harsh command. She took a big gulp of her coffee, hoping the caffeine would miraculously infuse her brain with the power to both stay awake and understand Statistics ... the most ridiculous required course ever. Having failed her first two times through the class, she hired Suzanne—a graduate student recommended by her professor—to tutor her through her third and hopefully final attempt.

"Yes, got it," Ava replied, trying to pull off a sorry-if-it-looked-like-I-was-ignoring-you-while-I-worked-on-the-problem attitude, but knowing she'd probably been staring at the page glassy-eyed and lost, per usual. "So ... um ... the probability is one-fifth."

"Not even close," Suzanne sighed. She put her head down on the table in frustration and defeat.

Ava didn't blame her. Tutoring her in statistics was no easy task. Her brain just wasn't wired to handle all of those numbers and logic, or at least that's what she'd convinced herself. She was a creative type, and years ago she'd heard her father telling someone you were either a numbers person or a creative person, never both. Since her father always spoke the truth, she took that to be her gospel. It was no wonder she was having so much trouble. Still, Wolfenson College didn't care about any of that. In order to graduate, she needed to pass this class; it was that simple, even if it wasn't remotely close to simple for her.

"Let's try again. I promise to pay attention this time. It's just been a really long day, and this subject is hard for me anyway." She closed her eyes for a moment thinking that must have been the biggest understatement in the history of the world. When she looked back at Suzanne, she said, "I don't even know why you care. You're getting paid either way."

Lifting her head, Suzanne shot her a contemptuous glare. "My reputation is at stake. This isn't working, Ava."

"Well, that's my fault, not yours. I just don't get this stuff. We're still working, so there's hope, right?

Don't worry about your reputation. I'm sure you'll have no problem finding other students to tutor. I'd be happy to put in a good word for you."

"You won't need to. Someone else has already hired me."

"That's great! More money in your pocket, and just in time for the holidays. I hope you're planning on getting me something nice." Ava's giggles faded to silence when she noticed that Suzanne wasn't laughing at her joke. Not that she ever laughed at her attempts at humor. She was generally all business, and Ava wondered if she was like this all the time, or if she had a softer side when she wasn't working. She was hard to read and never answered any of the personal questions Ava tried to sneak in to avoid working on lame math problems. In any event, her serious look seemed even more serious than usual.

"You're not understanding what I'm saying. What I mean is that someone hired me to tutor them *in place of you*. I guess what I'm trying to say is I'm firing you."

"You can't fire me," Ava stated matter-of-factly, wondering if she was having one of those weird dreams that happened when you'd sort of dozed off but weren't quite asleep. "I'm the one who hired you."

"Fine," Suzanne replied flatly. "Then I quit."

"But—you can't *quit*. I need you! If you leave, I'll fail again!"

"I hate to break it to you, but you're going to fail this class with or without me. You might as well save your money at this point and cut your losses. I honestly don't know what else to do for you. We can't even get past the basics, and the final is a week from tomorrow."

"You're saying I'm a lost cause? Please! You have to give me another chance. I'll pay you double. I'll even sit in with your other student. Just *please.* If I don't pass, I'll have to take it again, and they aren't even offering this class again in the spring." Ava shuddered. Just the thought of what might happen to her made her break out in a cold sweat. She took a deep breath and said the words she hoped would not become a reality, "If I fail, I won't be able to graduate on time." The thought of missing out on it and having to take Statistics for the fourth time—over the summer no less—was too much for her to handle. She felt the sting of tears in her eyes, felt them well up and spill over, sliding down her cheeks in jagged paths.

"Oh, all right," Suzanne snapped. "You can turn off the waterworks. You know you would have done much better as a drama major, don't you?"

It took all of the self-control she could muster to keep from rolling her eyes but, the last thing she needed to do was offend Suzanne. The only thing that mattered was that she was going to continue to tutor her.

"Honestly, I don't even know if I can help you at this point. Are you at least willing to take it seriously this time?"

She wiped her eyes and nodded.

"You're running out of chances, you know," Suzanne stated, packing up her books. "Meet me in the library on Saturday at one o'clock—and don't be late."

"Thank you," Ava said meekly. She waited for her tutor to leave the room, then pulled out her phone and called the gallery to let them know she would be missing work over the weekend. She hated to do it, but she hated the thought of failing Statistics even more.

She jumped, letting out a startled yelp when her phone rang again at the same moment she ended the call to her boss. Holly. *Finally*, Ava thought, clicking the talk button. The voice on the other end was yapping full steam ahead before she even had a chance to say hello.

"Sorry I couldn't call you right away. We were reviewing for exams, and I'm already so lost in this class it's not funny. Twentieth century literature, yuck! I don't know how you creative types can stand this stuff. I've got Calculus IV next. Now there's a class that makes sense. There's a right answer and a wrong answer, and a logical way to figure it out. Logic, Ava, simple logic. All that other stuff is just hokey bullshit if you ask me."

Ava laughed for the first time since— Well, she couldn't remember the last time. She could always count on her sisters to cheer her up, though some days it was hard to believe she and Holly were actually related.

"Tell you what. I'll take your literature exam for you, if you'll take my statistics test for me."

"I wish. Told you to transfer here last year when I started as a freshman, didn't I? At the very least we could have tutored each other. How's that going anyway?"

"Not good, but it's not the tutor, it's the subject. I think I might fail ... again."

"Is that why you sounded so down in your text?"

"No." Ava filled her in on art class and Carly's attempts at being ... funny? Come to think of it, she wasn't sure what Carly's intentions had been, but they most definitely hadn't been funny.

"Aw, hon, I'm sorry. She's probably just jealous because you were the one getting the attention, so she was being an ass. I mean, honestly, can you blame her? After all, the hottest of the Haines sisters is at Wolfenson College flaunting her stuff all over campus. How could she not be green with envy?"

"Uh huh." Hottest Haines sister... That's what her *sisters* said, but that didn't make it true – especially not on a campus filled with other 'hot' girls flaunting *their* stuff too. Here, she was just one of the crowd. "Didn't you say you had to get to geometry or something?"

"Actually it was Calculus IV, and yes, I do have to go. Feel better, sweets?"

"A little. You sure you don't want to switch places for exams?" Ava asked.

"Look, you're the one who wanted to go to a small school," Holly reminded her. "You could totally sit in on my literature exam here and no one would notice … you'd just be a number in my class of eighty. Unfortunately, I'm pretty sure your professor would notice when his beautiful, tall, brunette was suddenly replaced by a short, chubby blonde."

"You're not chubby, and you're not short," Ava corrected. "You're gorgeous."

"Gorgeous? I don't know about that. I'll rescind chubby, but I'm sticking with height challenged … especially when standing next to you. Plus, there's the dramatic difference in our hair color. My point is, even if we weren't four hours apart, we'd never get away with it. Not at Wolfenson anyway."

Ava sighed.

"Chill out, okay? I have faith in you. Beauty and brains … you can do it. Anyway, this week's meeting of our mutual admiration society needs to wrap up, because I really do have to run."

"Thanks, Holly. You'll do great too. Throw the logic out the window, and write from your heart. It works, trust me. Love you."

4

"Look, I said I was sorry, Ava. How long are you planning on staying mad at me?" Carly pouted as she raised a forkful of unidentifiable meat to her lips.

They were sitting at a table in the southwest corner of the student dining hall enjoying lunch. At least Carly seemed to be enjoying hers. Ava just pushed her salad around on her plate, unable to work up much of an appetite. She wished she didn't have to eat meals in the dining hall anymore. Wasn't that supposed to be one of the perks of being a senior? Getting the apartment, living off campus, eating normal food again? Unfortunately for her, she didn't have time most days to get back to her apartment between classes, and by the time she thought of packing her own lunch, she was usually running late. A gourmet-less meal in the cafeteria was generally the only option left if she didn't want to starve. Salad was typically a safe choice.

She took a sip of her iced tea. Almost two days had gone by, and she'd yet to speak to her friend. "Oh, I don't know, Carly, maybe *forever?*"

"Well, at least you're being reasonable," she responded, her voice so heavy with sarcasm Ava was surprised the words hadn't hit the floor with a crash.

She continued to make a swirling mixture of lettuce, chopped carrots, and salad dressing on her plate as her agitation grew. The more she twirled it, the more she thought it looked like a modern art painting she remembered studying in Professor Morey's class last semester. *Is this how the greats came up with their ideas?* she wondered. *Using food churned with emotion as their models?*

She'd planned on having a quick bite to eat alone today before heading to the studio to work on her project, when Carly plopped down in the chair across from her. It wasn't entirely unexpected as they ate lunch together almost every Friday, but Ava had hoped the cold shoulder treatment would have been enough to let her know she wasn't ready to talk yet.

"You went too far you know," she said, continuing the circular movements with her fork.

"Will you at least admit he's cute?" Carly raised her eyebrows, hoping to lighten the mood a little.

Of course he was cute, but she wasn't going to acknowledge it. Her stomach did a little flip as she thought about his hair, brown with natural red highlights. Highlights Ava paid good money to have put into her hair twice a year, hoping to achieve the same effect. As if that wasn't enough, the brown flecks in his incredible green eyes matched that perfect hair ... well, perfectly. She'd tried to avoid looking directly at him, but those eyes had made it nearly impossible not to notice. They drew her in with unspoken words— words she worked hard to ignore. But, it wasn't just those things she found attractive. Ava had always had a thing for lips—and his were amazing, full... and soft—at least she imagined that's how they would feel as they kissed ... no, she wasn't going there with this guy. She didn't care if he was cute, or that everything about him was straight off the proverbial tall, dark, and handsome checklist. Right now she needed to stay focused on what was important. Besides, all the cuteness in the world didn't erase arrogance.

"You're smiling. I knew it!" Carly sat back in her chair looking smug.

"Knew what? I haven't admitted anything, and I wasn't smiling. I was smirking. There's a difference."

"Oh really? Care to enlighten me?"

"I'd love to, but I have to run." She picked up her tray holding her barely eaten work of art, relieved that it was time to go.

"Wait! Do you want to hang out later?" Carly asked as Ava got to her feet.

"I don't think so." Her tone was curt, impatient, and the flash of pain in Carly's eyes made her feel the tiniest hint of guilt.

"You're still mad at me, really? I was just trying to be funny. Honest. I didn't mean anything by it. I swear on my favorite paintbrush and oils, I won't do it again. Forgive me?" Batting her eyelashes, she curled her lips back into a hesitant smile.

Ava sighed. While she knew she should still be mad at her friend, she didn't see the point. As much as she hated to admit it, Carly was just being Carly. It wasn't the first time she'd acted this way, and it wouldn't be the last.

"I can't. I've got to study for three classes and then head over to the gallery for work tonight. Don't you have finals too? They start on Monday, you know."

"I already finished my Art History paper, and most of my portfolio projects." Carly grinned. "I only have two sketches to touch up for Senaca's class due Wednesday. We're not all double majors like you. What about after work? Sounds like you'll need a drink by then."

"Probably," Ava agreed. "Or sleep. I'm not sure which one I'll want more when eleven o'clock rolls around."

"Why are you working so late? I thought the gallery closed at nine-thirty on Fridays. Is there an opening tonight you forgot to tell me about? You aren't still mad at me are you?"

"No and no. The next big exhibit we have is that photography one coming up next Friday right after exams. The one called Images in Flight. I told you about it, remember?"

"Oh yeah, the one where the crazy guy flies an airplane and takes pictures of the ground at the same time."

"Sort of. It's not like he's thirty-thousand feet up in the air and hanging out the window with one hand on the controls or anything, but yeah." Ava paused, wondering how it was Thomas Malloy actually managed to take those photos without crashing the plane. "Anyway, I can't work tomorrow, and with the exhibit coming up soon, I'm putting in some extra time tonight."

"What's going on tomorrow? Hot date?"

"Yeah, if you call a study session with Suzanne, my statistics tutor, a hot date."

Carly shuddered. "Um, no. If that's your definition of a hot date, you need more help than I thought."

"Who says I need help?"

"Wow, you really are stressed, aren't you? I'm just messing with you."

"My statistics exam is one week from today—the morning of the opening. I've got get my ass in gear if I want to pass this thing."

"You should consider that drink tonight. It'll do you good."

"I guess," she said, relenting after a moment's indecision. "A little fun might be just what I need before buckling down. All right. Come by the gallery at eleven. I really do have to run. See you later."

5

A va had only been working at the Main Street Gallery for six months, yet Cynthia Simms, the owner, seemed to value her opinion—more than her own at times. At first, she thought her boss was just testing her young intern, and perhaps she had been. However, she'd always appeared satisfied with her responses. There was no doubt that the openings and exhibits were always a success, much of it due to Ava's keen eye for arrangement.

Over the short time she'd been working there, Cynthia had promoted her from gofer, to file clerk, to artistic assistant—all unpaid, of course. This was, after all, an internship for college credit. Regardless, each time Ava was given more responsibilities and independence, a new intern was brought in to take over her previous duties.

As far as she could tell, she was the only student Cynthia showed any real interest in. She was also the only one trusted to handle openings. A first in the history of the gallery since interns normally only worked during the day and behind the scenes.

Securing a position like this was no easy task. While there were plenty of art galleries in the quaint college town, Main Street internships were the most coveted, as Cynthia Simms was known in the industry as one of the major players and was able to bring in some big name artists. She was quite selective about who she accepted to the program, and she rarely gave her students any real responsibilities ... that is until last spring.

Ava impressed her during her interview, not only because she was pursuing a dual degree, but also because she had done her research. She knew all about her prospective new boss and what exhibits had recently come through, as well as which ones were scheduled over the next few weeks.

Cynthia had been intrigued. However, what really captured her attention was when Ava suggested adjusting an overhead spotlight—just slightly—to accentuate a painting. At first, she was put off by her moxie, but had given in and humored her. The difference had been stunning, and she 'hired' Ava on the spot.

"What do you think about this, my dear?" Cynthia was asking. Ava shook her head, letting the memories drift away as she looked at the photographs before her.

She took a step back and studied the arrangement with a practiced eye. With the exhibit just one week away, she wanted to make sure everything would be perfect. "I think the meadows should be to the right of the lake, with the mountains as the showcase piece." She stepped to the left slightly. "Yes, definitely. It should be the first thing patrons see as they enter through the doors."

Her boss tilted her head, trying to notice what her intern was seeing so clearly. She nodded. "Yes... Yes, you're absolutely right." She promptly switched the photocopies around. "Of course." She slipped into the alcove as Ava marked her clipboard with the approved layout.

A deep voice startled her, "I agree."

"I'm sorry, sir, we're closed," Ava murmured, turning to face the man. She wished the gallery had a bell for the front door. It would be nice to know when a customer walked in, but Cynthia was against having one. She thought it would disturb the zen-like atmosphere she was trying to create. This late in the evening, it shouldn't have even been an issue anyway. The doors should have been locked hours ago.

"No, no, it's all right," Cynthia said, hurrying back to stand beside her. "This is Thomas Malloy, our esteemed photographer. I forgot to mention that he'd be stopping by to drop off some promotional materials. Thomas, this is my intern, Ava. I didn't realize that the two of you hadn't met yet."

"Oh," Ava said, a nervous smile forming across her mouth. "I'm so sorry. It's a pleasure to meet you, sir. Your work is wonderful ... really. I'm a big fan. We're so very excited to have your exhibit here. It's great." She clamped her lips together to stop the endless stream of words from escaping, took a deep breath, and trying to pretend she was the professional she strove to be, apologized. "I'm sorry, I'm babbling. Sometimes I get a little star struck when I meet the artists."

Thomas laughed a strong, sexy, laugh. Ava couldn't help but notice his mouth—his sensual lips curved in an amused smiled. She wondered what it would be like to—

No!

She needed to stay focused. School. Work. Graduation. And definitely not one of Cynthia's clients. She took a deep breath to calm herself.

"I'm flattered, but the pleasure is mine," he said with a cultured English accent that made her knees weak. Holding his hand out, she expected him to shake hers when she offered it in return. She had to bite back a sigh when he pressed his soft lips against the back of it instead. When he finally released her, she felt chilled. "Cynthia says tells me you have a real gift for displaying art. From what I just witnessed, I'm inclined to agree."

"Oh," she stammered. She tried desperately not to sound like a silly schoolgirl with a crush. "It's easy when I have great pieces to work with, Mr. Malloy." *Cringe.*

"We'll have none of this Mr. Malloy business. Please, call me Thomas."

Before Ava could respond, another voice interrupted her.

"You know the door's not locked— Oh, I'm sorry, am I interrupting? You did tell me to come at eleven, didn't you, Ava?" Carly practically bounced into the gallery wearing a tight fitting, low cut, and very short, sequined dress that sparkled beneath the bright overhead lights.

Where exactly were they going for that drink, a strip club? Not to mention the fact that it was December, and she wasn't wearing a coat. Ava felt a little under-dressed in a comfortable blue sweater and slacks, until she noticed Thomas giving her friend a strange look.

"Right," he said, clearing his throat. "Well, Cynthia, I've got those extra postcards you've asked for, as well as business cards, and some other miscellaneous promotional items. Also, the photos for the opening will be delivered in the next day or so. I can see my exhibit is in very capable hands." He nodded to Ava and smiled. "I was going to see if you and Cynthia wanted to join me for a late cocktail, but I see you already have other plans." He looked pointedly at Carly with that strange look again.

"Oh, Thomas, darling," Cynthia replied with a dramatic sigh. "Can we make it another time? I'm afraid I must get my beauty sleep tonight. It's been a very long day, and I'm not going to have my star intern to help in the gallery tomorrow." Cynthia reached out and touched Ava on the shoulder, showing her she didn't mind much.

"Ah, big plans this weekend?" Thomas asked, looking at Ava.

"No, I've just got to study. Finals are coming up this week." Why did his questions make her so uncomfortable?

"Oh how I remember those days. I'm not as old as I look you know," he said, winking.

Ava wondered exactly how old he was. If she had to guess, she'd say early forties or late thirties. "You don't look that old. I mean ..." She laughed nervously, feeling the heat rise to her cheeks.

"What she means is that there's no reason you can't come out with us tonight," Carly blurted out in typical Carly fashion. "We were just going out for a drink. Isn't that right, Ava?"

6

"What?" Carly looked at Ava from across the table as they waited for their drinks to arrive.

She swallowed a sigh and took a slow look around the crowded, noisy bar. They'd been lucky to get a table tonight. Weekends—especially after dark— were always crazy at The Corner Spot, especially when school was in session. Securing a stool at the bar was usually considered a major score, but a whole table? That didn't happen often. Thomas, who had ordered the first round of drinks, had promptly excused himself to make a quick phone call and had stepped back outside.

"Well, let me see now. First you come to the gallery looking like you forgot to put on half of your outfit—"

"You don't like my dress?" Carly asked, batting her eyelashes.

"You look like a glitter factory exploded on you. And you … um, forgot to cover some important parts," Ava said. She knew she was being a bit rude and overly dramatic, but she was annoyed with the way her friend had crossed the line with her client.

Carly opened her mouth as if she were about to speak, but shut it as the drinks were delivered to the table.

"Then," Ava continued once the waitress left, "you invited my client out with us for a drink. And not just anywhere, mind you. You invited him to The Spot. *Our Spot.*"

"For the record," Carly said, "he invited us out first."

"Correction. He invited Cynthia and me out—for a business drink—and Cynthia declined, remember? Nowhere in there did he extend the invitation to you."

"Well, it was obvious we already had plans, so I just assumed I was part of the deal. And what's wrong with coming here?"

She took a drink of her rum and coke and continued, "Because this is where we all come to unwind—as students—where I don't need to be Ava Haines, assistant to Cynthia Simms of the Main Street

Gallery. Now with Thomas here, this has become a social drink, not a business drink."

"And that's a problem why?" Carly asked, smirking. "Don't be mad at me. Just have fun!"

She smiled and shook her head. She loved Carly, she really did. She wouldn't be sitting here if she didn't. Just sometimes... It's just one night— One uncomfortable night. *You can handle this.*

"Sorry about that, ladies," Thomas said as he approached the table, flashing them a grin and a mouthful of brilliant white teeth. He took the seat across from Ava. "Excellent, I see the drinks have arrived." Taking a long swallow of the imported beer he'd ordered, he closed his eyes in near ecstasy, then asked, "It looked like the two of you were having a lively conversation. Anything I might find interesting?"

"Oh, just boring school stuff," Ava said with a defensive tone. "That's kind of what we do here. It probably seems dull for anyone who's not a student. Hey!" She kicked Carly back under the table, only harder.

"Oh, I don't know about that, so far I'm finding you both quite entertaining." He smiled, his gaze lingering on Ava's face so long; she felt color flood her cheeks. Carly looked back and forth between them, then grinned and jumped to her feet.

"Hey, that's Melanie from the sculpture class we took last year." She pointed to a girl standing at the bar. A girl who didn't look the least bit familiar. "I haven't talked to her in ages."

"Wait! You're leaving?" Ava asked in disbelief. The last thing she wanted was to be left alone with a virtual stranger.

"Hardly. We've only been here five minutes. I'm just going to say hello to an old friend. I'll be back. Besides, you two have business stuff to go over. If I don't get to talk to you later, Thomas, thanks for the drink."

"What do you mean if you don't get to talk to him later? I thought you said you were coming back," Ava accused, trying to keep the panic out of her voice.

"I don't know, things could happen. That guy Melanie is standing next to is kind of cute." She winked as she walked off.

"Carly! Wait." She shook her head frantically, but Carly turned and danced her way to the bar, not glancing back even once. They were definitely going to have to set some ground rules for situations like this, number one on the list being going AWOL in the future will be strictly prohibited.

"Looks like it's just us," Thomas said, running one finger in slow patterns in the condensation on his bottle. He still hadn't taken his eyes off her. Ava swallowed hard.

"Sorry about that. Carly can be kind of unpredictable sometimes." She twirled the stick in her drink, wishing desperately that Thomas would finish his beer and leave. "You don't have to stay, you know. I can have Cynthia call you on Monday if you need to discuss the details of your exhibit."

"There's no need to apologize. I'm glad Carly invited me. I'd be terribly bored all alone otherwise. We might as well stay and have our drinks. So tell me, have you always loved art?"

She took a long sip of her drink. Partly to calm her nerves, and partly to remind herself that as good looking as Thomas was, he was Cynthia's client. No matter how casual this might feel, she needed to be on her best professional behavior.

"I have," she admitted. "It's been my passion for as long as I can remember. Have you always loved photography?"

"Indeed. My parents bought me my first camera when I was just toddling around back in London. One of those fake plastic ones, mind you, but according to them, I never let it out of my sight. When I was seven or eight years old, I started a dog walking business in my neighborhood to earn money. I saved every penny to buy my first real camera." His eyes seemed to glow with excitement as he shared the story, and Ava knew how he felt. It was precisely how she felt about her career as well.

"And was it the same with flying? Did you always love to fly?"

"Heavens no, I hate to fly! In fact, when my parents decided to move to this side of the Atlantic, I was so terrified of the plane ride, they had to tranquilize me. It was quite humiliating given I was fifteen at the time," Thomas told her with a hearty laugh.

"But your exhibit is called Images in Flight. Didn't you take the photos while flying?" She asked, confused.

"Yes, that was a crazy idea I came up with one night when I'd had a bit too much scotch, I'm afraid. I was in a quaint little pub with some friends. One happened to be a pilot and convinced me to go up in his two-seat Cessna that weekend with my camera. I did get some amazing shots, but I never want to do anything like that again. I don't quite have the stomach for it."

"Oh, that makes more sense," Ava said, trying to hold in a giggle.

"More sense than what?" He seemed to be amused over her reaction.

She realized too late that she probably shouldn't tell him, but the effects of the alcohol were setting in, and she was feeling more relaxed.

"Well, when I was first telling Carly about your exhibit, we thought you were flying the plane and taking the photos at the same time. I pictured you hanging out the window with one hand on the controls and the other on the camera."

"Ah, I was a daredevil, eh? Well that sounds much sexier than vomiting into an airsick bag at ten-thousand feet in between photos now doesn't it? I won't tell if you don't. Deal?" Thomas lifted up his bottle.

"Deal," Ava agreed, her glass meeting it in midair with a clink.

7

As expected, the library was packed. It was, after all, the weekend before final exams. Luckily, most of Ava's classes were ones in which she had to just hand in art projects. Those she had under control, leaving only Statistics to worry about. Statistics. Just the word made her entire body break out in a cold sweat. It was an evil word for a useless class. There was only one equation she needed to solve— The probability that she would pass the class. Hopefully it was sixty-five percent or better.

She'd forgotten to ask Suzanne where exactly to meet in the library. It wasn't like she was familiar with the building. Studying and Ava didn't actually go hand in hand. She spent most of her time on campus in class or at the gallery—where she had high hopes Cynthia would offer her a full-time position after graduation. *If* she graduated. *Damn Statistics.*

Bauer Hall, the official name of the library, was an exquisite building, as were most of the buildings on Wolfenson's quaint campus. The exterior was made of the granite and limestone found in the local quarries back in the late 1800s. The interior was five floors comprised of a maze of passageways. Private study rooms were set between stacks of books, tables, and cubicles. All of the floors were joined together by an elaborate and winding center staircase, topped by an extravagant chandelier that spanned nearly the entire opening. To someone not familiar with the layout, the building could prove to be quite overwhelming.

Ava's phone vibrated from where she'd tucked it in her pocket. Maybe it was Suzanne finally answering one of her texts about where to meet.

Ava, would love to continue our conversation. Dinner tonight? – Thomas

She couldn't help but wonder how he got her number. She'd headed home shortly after she and Thomas finished their drinks, explaining she'd booked early morning studio time. It hadn't been a lie, but that had never kept her from staying out late before. The truth was she'd worried about what might happen with Thomas after another drink or two. Had it been anyone other than one of Cynthia's high profile clients, she would have stayed. Well, not anyone else. Not that arrogant guy from art class. Carly, who was still at the bar flirting with some boy when Ava left, must have given him her number. *Great.*

Deciding Thomas wasn't a priority, she ignored the text. Right now, she needed to get to her tutoring session. She searched each floor, hoping to get a glimpse of Suzanne's perfectly coiffed blonde hair. Finally, she spotted her sitting at a third floor table.

"You're late," Suzanne said, barely looking up from her pile of books.

"You didn't tell me where to meet you," Ava reminded her, trying her best to sound more apologetic and less annoyed. "I was here at one o'clock, but it took me ten minutes to find you." She looked around. "I thought you said someone else was coming."

"He'll be here any minute. I figured you wouldn't be here on time, so I told him to come at one-fifteen," her tutor said smugly.

"Thanks for the vote of confidence," she muttered under her breath, pulling out a chair to sit down. Restraining herself from further comment, she removed her Statistics book from her backpack, and opened to the page where they left off earlier in the week.

"Well, I was right, wasn't I? Here he comes ... early, too. Maybe you can learn something from him."

"Well, you probably told him where to meet—" Ava sunk into her seat mid-sentence, wishing she could sink into the floor. It was ... *him*.

"Hello Max," Suzanne said. "This is the student I told you about. Ava Haines, meet Max Wallis."

So it was Max, not Mark or Matt. She knew it started with an M. He looked Ava straight in the eyes, but she couldn't tell if he recognized her or not. Maybe, if she was lucky, he wouldn't remember her. "Nice to meet you," she said, deciding to go the 'I have no idea who you are' route.

"Actually, we've met before, but I guess you don't recognize me with my clothes on," he replied, smiling as he took a seat across from her.

Shit.

"Great ... one of your *friends*, Ava?" Suzanne asked, her upper lip curled in disgust.

"What? No! I mean, we don't actually *know* each other," Ava insisted.

"Whatever. What you do on your own time is your own business," Suzanne mocked. She leaned in close to Ava and with a loud whisper added, "But you should at least get their names."

"Ugh! No! It's not like that. Ew! He was just one of the nude models for my art class. Nothing special or anything. I mean, he was fine— I mean, he was okay— I mean— Can we talk about statistics please?"

Ava glanced down at her book, propped her elbow on the table, and cupped her hand over her eyebrows like a visor to block out their stares, yet she could feel their eyes on her. Over two thousand students at this college ... two-freaking-thousand students. What were the odds that he would be the one to show up for her joint tutoring session? Of course, if she were paying attention to what Suzanne was saying right now instead of hovering on the verge of a panic attack, she might be able to answer that question. She needed air. She needed to call Holly. She needed to find an excuse to leave—now—but she couldn't. She needed someone to teach her this stuff. She needed to pass Statistics. She needed to breathe.

"Actually, now that I think about it, I think it's a great idea. What do you think, Ava?" Suzanne asked.

She looked up. Crap. She knew she had to agree. If she didn't, she'd be minus a tutor before "I'm sorry, what did you say," finished leaving her mouth, and that just wasn't an option. "Um, sure. Sounds good to me," she replied.

Max smiled. Double crap.

"Perfect. I really think this might be exactly what you need. A fresh perspective. It'll be a win-win for all of us."

8

"Quit staring at me, will you? I'm trying to figure out these problems." Ava glanced up from her paper, meeting Max's eyes. *Ignore him. Just ignore him*, she told herself, looking back down at the book.

Apparently, Suzanne's *plan* had been to reserve one of the private study rooms in the library for Ava and Max, to allow them to work through their assigned statistics problems *alone* before meeting back with them at four o'clock. She wished she'd been paying closer attention because she'd never have agreed to being cooped up in a room with this guy. Wasn't she paying *Suzanne* to tutor her? How was she supposed to learn anything on her own? Okay, so she wasn't on her own, but she was paying to be with Suzanne, not Max.

"I'm not staring. I'm watching. There's a difference. You do realize you've been looking at your paper for ten minutes, and you haven't written one thing down. Do you want me to help you?"

"I don't need your help!"

"Sorry, I'm just trying to be nice. I'm pretty good with some of this," he offered again.

"Doubt it. Anyway, last I checked you hired my tutor also."

"Wow. You're strung a little tight, eh?"

"Excuse me?" Ava glared at Max. Of course she was a little on edge. Besides the fact that she was stuck here with *him*, she actually needed to learn something this time. And why did he always have that grin on his face? *That damn sexy grin.*

"You just seem a bit stressed out, that's all," he said, wisely rewording his statement.

Ava pushed her chair back, hitting the wall behind her with a thud. Rising to her feet, she began to pace. "I'm not stressed." Okay, she was, but she wasn't about to let him know that.

"To be honest, you're kind of distracting me from my own work."

"I'm distracting you," she repeated more as a statement than a question. She couldn't help but feel the hostility rise in her voice. Who did he think he was?

"Yeah," he said, starting to sound annoyed. "Ever since you got here, you've been sighing, tapping, mumbling to yourself, and making all kinds of disrupting sounds. I mean, look at you now ... you can't stop pacing, and your phone keeps buzzing. Someone is apparently desperate to get in touch with you."

She stopped and picked up her phone. There were six texts. One each from Holly and Tessa—Holly checking in to make sure she was feeling better, and Tessa to ask for advice about her latest crush. A third was from Carly, asking how it went last night and warning her that she gave Thomas her number. The last three were from Thomas—one with a couple of questions about the exhibit, one asking her what type of food she liked in the event the she did accept his dinner invitation, and one wondering if he actually had the right number since he hadn't gotten any texts back. He also apologized to whomever he was texting in case it was a wrong number. With the afternoon she was having, maybe going out with Thomas tonight wasn't such a bad idea. After all, he did have questions about the exhibit, and it was only dinner.

"In fact," he continued, "I never would have agreed to share my tutoring sessions with you if I knew what a pain you were going to be."

"A pain?" Ava put her phone down. "Me? I'll tell you what's a pain. This class. It's stupid. What do I even need it for?" She stopped pacing and walked over to Max, who was now standing as well.

"From what Suzanne tells me, you're trying to avoid round four in order to graduate," he said, smirking.

Ouch. Whatever.

She couldn't remember the last time she'd met someone so rude and arrogant ... and hot. *Why did he have to be so hot?* She was trying to think of something witty to say, when he began to speak again.

"So what's your major anyway? Art students don't need Statistics, do they?" he asked.

"I'm a dual art and business major," she replied, hands on her hips.

"Pretty, talented, and smart ... I like that."

"Wow, you're smooth. Is that how you work? First you insult a girl, then you compliment her?" She wondered why guys always thought that line would cause a girl to melt. If anything, his eyes and lips would cause her to melt. She tried to shake off the thought. "So what's your story? Playgirl Magazine requiring a minimum GPA these days?"

"Funny ... I forgot to add funny to my list. Actually, I'm trying to make some extra money so I can go to flight school after graduation."

"What is it with me and guys with airplanes?" Ava mumbled with a short, harsh laugh.

"Yeah? You've got a thing for that?"

"Actually, no."

"Too bad. Anyway, I'm a business major also. My parents said I needed a backup plan. I'm surprised we haven't had any other classes together."

"Maybe we have, and I just didn't notice. I don't really pay attention in my business classes. They bore me," Ava admitted.

"That would explain why you're about to fail Statistics, wouldn't it? Usually when I'm bored in class, I study the people around me. I'm sure I would have remembered you. Then again, I tend to pay attention to the subject matter in my classes."

She rolled her eyes. *Apparently not, or he wouldn't need tutoring.* "So far I haven't run across anyone worth noticing."

"Well, I couldn't help but notice you noticing me in art class." Max moved closer, a little too close, and she backed up … but only slightly.

"That's because I had to draw you, remember? If I hadn't looked at you, I wouldn't have been able to complete the assignment."

"I believe the term the teacher used was *gawking*," he reminded her.

"Are you always this *charming*?" Ava asked. He was close enough now that she could feel his warm breath soft against her face. Her heart started to race, and she ran her tongue over her lips, nervous.

"Are you always this *sarcastic*?"

Max didn't wait for an answer as he pushed her body against the wall, finding her waiting lips.

9

"Are you kidding me?" Suzanne stood in the doorway of the study room, arms crossed, the sound of her voice startling Ava and Max mid-kiss.

"Suzanne!" Ava took a step to the side and wiped the corners of her mouth.

"I thought I'd check in a little early, see how you were doing," she said, clearly annoyed. She reached down and picked up the blank pieces of paper, waving them slowly in the air before slapping them back down on the table. She looked back over to Ava and Max, now standing about three feet apart, looking everywhere but at each other. "I felt kind of bad leaving you two alone like that—since you were paying

me and all. I thought maybe you might need some
help. But I can see you really don't need my help at
all. In fact, I was right about you all along, Ava.
You're a lost cause."

"No, I'm not like that!" She felt the tears in her
eyes and glanced at Max, desperate for his help.

"Don't blame Ava for this. I started—" he began to
say, but Suzanne cut him off with her next words.

"Save it," she said. "I'm wasting my time with both
of you. I could be studying for my own exams right
now. I don't need this crap." She reached into her
pocket and pulled out the money Ava and Max paid
her earlier. "Here you go. A full refund for today's
session. I'd keep it, but it would just make me feel ...
dirty." She shuddered and flung the money on the
table. Just before she stepped into the main room of
the library, turning around, she said, "I'd tell you it's
been a pleasure, but it really hasn't. See you two ...
never."

"Suzanne! Wait!" Ava called, running after her.
Unfortunately, it was too late. Suzanne was already
lost among the stacks of books. Groups of students
studying at nearby tables glanced up, letting Ava
know by their expressions that she needed to keep her
voice down.

It wouldn't have mattered. She could have shouted
herself hoarse. There was no way Suzanne would agree
to come back now anyway. She stormed back into the
room, where Max stood by the table, and slammed the

door behind her. Screw the people studying out there. She didn't care if the noise echoed all through the building. She was angry, and she wasn't about to allow the people out there be privy to the next few moments, that was for damn sure.

"Just great!" Ava cried, flinging her arms around as she spoke. Max took a few steps back, probably afraid she might smack him – and she was tempted. Oh so tempted. "I hope you're happy. This is all your fault."

"Actually, I don't think it was *all* my fault. If I recall, you seemed to be enjoying yourself ... or was I mistaken, because I'm pretty sure I wasn't imagining your hands on my—"

"All right, all right. I get it. For the record, my hands were on your back the entire time."

"Uh huh," he smiled.

"What am I going to do?" She leaned against the wall—her shoulders slumped. "I'm going to fail Statistics ... again!"

"Not if you let me help you, which is really all I was trying to do to begin with, remember?"

"How are you going to do that when you're here to get tutored too? And why aren't you freaking out?"

"Suzanne's plan, remember?"

She shook her head. "No, I don't. I wasn't actually listening when she set that whole thing up. Care to refresh my memory?"

"Shocking," he said, gasping dramatically before he grinned again. "Do you think maybe you can pay attention this time?"

"Just tell me what she had in mind, and how it's supposed to help me. Without the commentary please."

"Okay, okay, calm down. Suzanne thought it would be a good idea for us to work together because she was getting frustrated trying to help you on her own. Honestly, I can see why."

Ava rolled her eyes. "Without. The. Commentary. Can we get on with the plan part?" she asked again, this time with clenched teeth and without the please.

"The *plan* was for me to help you. I'm in Advanced Statistics, and you're still struggling with basic concepts. Suzanne thought having someone else explain it to you in a different way might work."

"Wait a minute. Let me get this straight. You take ... *Advanced Statistics*? On purpose? Ew, why?"

Max dropped his head, blowing a long breath out, before returning his gaze to Ava. "Now who's throwing in commentary? Did anyone ever tell you you're impossible to talk to? Cute, but impossible."

Ava raised her eyebrows and smiled. "Sorry. Just go on. Please."

"So the plan was, I would tutor you under Suzanne's supervision, and she would tutor me. Well, it seems we've lost the Suzanne part of the equation, but I can still teach you if you're interested. Of course, that doesn't help me out, but I'm sure there's another grad student somewhere on campus who needs to earn a little money for the holidays."

Was he serious? She stood with her hands on her hips, not knowing what to think. The kiss was still fresh on her mind, but so was the fear of failing. Her phone began to buzz yet *again.* She pulled it out of her pocket.

Hi. Still not sure if I have the right number, but if this is you, Ava, and you need a break from studying, I've got a table for two reserved at 7:00 at Habaneros. I heard you like Mexican food. – Thomas

"So do we have a deal or not?" Max asked, suddenly all business. Ava's skin was still tingling despite everything that had happened in the past few minutes. How could he just turn passion on and off so easily?

"What exactly was that before … with that kiss?" Ava asked, not quite ready to make a decision yet. She put the phone on her pile of books, still on the table.

"Look, I apologize, that shouldn't have happened. It was completely my fault. I know we got off on the wrong foot, and I can assure you that we *will* just study from now on. I know how important this exam is to you."

She didn't know if she should feel disappointed or relieved, but she knew she had a critical exam coming up and was out of options. It was time to get her priorities in order. She stuck out her hand. "Deal. But for studying, that's all. Got it?"

"Got it," Max agreed, accepting her handshake. "How's two tomorrow? I should probably head over to the Graduate School before it gets too late to see about getting myself a tutor."

She nodded. "Good luck. I'll see you tomorrow. And thanks."

10

Ava walked through the door of the restaurant, not really sure what she was doing there. After her *interesting* afternoon with Max, she supposed she needed to unwind for a bit. But with Thomas? He was a client ... Cynthia's client. While her employer had never specifically said she couldn't date one of the artists, she hadn't said she could either. Not that this was a date. *Was it?*

No. It couldn't be. Thomas was only looking to have some questions about the exhibit answered. But— Did people actually *have* business meetings at Habaneros? She supposed she was capable of keeping this strictly business—until the end of the exhibit.

There was always time for pleasure later, and two weeks wasn't that far away. Except she'd be going home then. Oh, who was she kidding? She deserved a *little* fun, right?

Shaking her head, she realized she was being ridiculous. Thomas was simply a nice older gentleman. He would probably be mortified if he knew the direction her thoughts were taking. *But what if it was a date?*

Ava hated when her brain played this type of back and forth with her. How was she supposed to make a rational decision with so many thoughts going through her head? She wished Holly had answered the phone when she tried to call her earlier, though she had a feeling her advice would have been along the lines of *go out with Thomas for dinner, then have Max for dessert.* That was definitely *not* happening.

The fact of the matter was, she'd been better off hanging out with Carly. They could have gone back to The Spot, had a couple of beers, and watched whatever band was on tap for the night. Carly would have flirted with some guy, and Ava would have played wingman, or wingwoman in her case. Then at some point, she would have headed home. *Alone.* Of course, then she'd be stuck eating a burger or chicken fingers for dinner, instead of the fine cuisine she was about to enjoy. She hoped Thomas was still here. She hadn't been able to bring herself to text him back, waiting for a call from Holly right up to the last minute.

She looked around the dimly lit restaurant. Habaneros had an intimate feel to it and was comprised largely of small tables for two. Most were occupied by couples sitting close, whispering secrets, smiling, and laughing. Mariachi-style music played softly in the background, drowning out any conversations taking place, as if to assure any discussions occurring would remain private.

Ava had only eaten at Habaneros once before. It wasn't exactly a restaurant that a college student could afford to frequent. The one time she had been there was when her Dad brought her for her pre-admittance interview back when she was in high school. They'd stuck out like a sore thumb, her dad in his customary flannel shirt and jeans, while Ava sported the new Wolfenson College sweatshirt she'd picked up that afternoon from the campus bookstore. Nothing screamed small town hicks like the two of them had that day.

She remembered that it had been a Tuesday night, and the maître d' who'd attempted to tell them they had no open tables, couldn't pull it off since the restaurant had been empty. Still, he led them to a table in the far corner of the restaurant out of sight from well … no one, since they had the place to themselves. She recalled the look on her dad's face when he'd looked at the menu. Talk about sticker shock. She'd asked if he wanted to go somewhere else, but knew his pride wouldn't allow that. Instead, she'd made sure to find the least expensive thing to order. The next time they came to the campus—the day her parents had dropped her off at school—they'd grabbed a burger at a diner near campus.

As Ava scanned the main dining area for Thomas, she wondered if he would be taking care of the bill for this meal. She certainly hoped so, seeing as her job at the gallery was a non-paying one.

"Ava, I'm glad you made it," the familiar voice said.

Feeling a light touch on her shoulder, she turned around, glancing up at Thomas who stood almost a full foot taller than her. She felt tingles race across her skin when he gently brushed her arm, helping her remove her coat.

"You look lovely," he said, eyeing the dark green dress she'd changed into when she'd decided to accept his invitation.

"Thank you," she replied. "So do you."

Whoa. Did she just tell a man he looked lovely? Well, he kind of did. Thomas Malloy had a certain style about him. While the sandy blond hair and dark eyes were enough to make her swoon, he was also rugged, put together, and artsy. He was wearing a dark sport coat over a dress shirt, with no tie, and casual pants—an outfit that normally looked nerdy to Ava. However, in this case, it worked. Maybe it was because he was older and had a more experienced look about him. Not fatherly old, but sophisticated old ... mature.

More importantly, not immature like Max. She shook her head to get the thought of her new tutor completely out of her head. She was here with Thomas.

"We're right over here." He led her to a table near the front window. Holding out her chair, he said, "I wanted to make sure I could see you come in since I didn't actually know if you'd be here or not. I see I had the right phone number after all."

"Yes," Ava said, biting the tip of one perfectly manicured fingernail. "I'm sorry. I got all of your texts. I just didn't have a chance to reply. It was a really strange afternoon." She sat down as he eased her chair in beneath her, before taking his own seat.

"Strange? How so?" He rested an arm on the edge of the table and leaned closer. It seemed as though she had his rapt attention.

She shook her head. She'd rather not relive those hours again ... especially when she was sitting here with a handsome Englishman. Instead, she said, "Intense and busy, and then ... confusing. Just a weird mix-up. It's all under control now."

He seemed to be about to say something, but a woman dressed in traditional Mexican attire stopped at the table with two large margaritas and a basket of tortilla chips.

"Thank you." Thomas nodded at her. After placing them down, she handed them a couple of menus that had been tucked under her arm and said she'd be back in a few minutes. "I hope you don't mind, but I took the liberty of ordering a drink for you. I thought you might be ready for one when you got here."

"But you didn't even know if I'd be coming," Ava replied.

"Well, I figured if you didn't show, I'd need that extra drink to drown my sorrows."

11

"No thanks," Ava said when the waitress returned to ask if she'd like to see the dessert menu. "I couldn't eat another bite." She finished her margarita in a final gulp. "Everything was delicious. Thank you. I'm just going to use the ladies room." As she stood, the entire room swayed. She'd only gotten up ten minutes earlier to answer a call from Tessa, when the third drink had arrived but felt nothing more than her usual buzz. "Or maybe I should sit for a few minutes. I think that last one might have been one too many."

"Should I bring the check, sir?" the waitress asked, glancing back and forth between them.

"Yes," Thomas replied, "and a couple of coffees, please."

"Certainly."

He looked at Ava with a concerned expression. "Are you okay?"

"Yes, yes. I'll be fine. I didn't realize those drinks were so strong. At The Spot I can usually handle more than three. Of course, there they probably don't use as much booze in each one, which would explain why they don't charge as much." She leaned across the table as far as she could, her hair nearly dipping in his water glass, and whispered loudly, "Have you seen the prices here?"

She slid back into her own seat just as the waitress returned with the coffee and check.

"Thanks," Thomas said, smiling.

"Yes," Ava agreed, maybe with a little more enthusiasm than was necessary. "Thank you so *very* much."

The waitress gave her an odd look before walking away.

She slurped her coffee. "Wow! This is great. You should try it!" Noticing Thomas pulling out his wallet, she added, "Oh, is it time to pay? Should I pay for mine? Because we didn't really discuss that before I got here."

"No, Ava, it's on me," Thomas softly said, no doubt trying to get her to lower the volume on her voice to match his, "but I think maybe it's time to get you home."

"Aw, you're just the sweetest man ever. But I think I should wait for the room to stop moving before I drive home. Is the room moving for you?"

"No, and you're not driving anywhere. I'll take you, and we'll come back for your car tomorrow."

She watched as Thomas threw a few hundred-dollar bills on the table, as if they were pennies. "Wow! That's a lot of green!"

He put his wallet back in his pocket and said, "Come on, you can lean on my arm."

Ava fumbled for her keys when they arrived at her apartment. For her entire life she'd had roommates. Growing up, she'd had to share a room with Holly, then as a freshman she'd been put into a triple. She'd kept the same two roommates her sophomore year, and moved into a house her junior year where she wound up having even more roommates. By the time she'd become a senior, she was ready to live on her own. So when she'd found the one bed studio, she'd grabbed it.

Now that she found herself alone with Thomas on the threshold of her apartment, she wished she had roommates again.

"Well, thank you, Thomas," she said, trying hard not to slur her words. "I appreciate you helping me make it home safely."

Ava desperately tried to guide her key toward the keyhole in the door, but was unable to make contact.

"Please, let me." He took them from her unsteady hand, swiftly unlocking and opening the door.

"Thank you ... again," she replied. "I think I'm good now. I appreciate—"

She slapped her hand over her mouth, her eyes popping wide open in dismay when she realized what was about to happen. She barely made it to the bathroom as the bile made its way up her throat. Dropping to her knees, she heaved numerous times.

Several long minutes passed before she was convinced it was safe to stand back up. She splashed water on her face, brushed her teeth, and prayed that Thomas had left her apartment. She cautiously peeked out of the bathroom only to find her prayers had been in vain.

"What are you doing?" Ava asked, watching as he stood in her tiny kitchen filling a pot with water.

"I'm making tea. I know you Americans prefer coffee, but we already tried that and look what happened. Now we're going to do things my way."

"I really think I'm okay. I just need some sleep. Thanks again for bringing me home. Sorry for the weird ending to the evening, and don't worry about my car. I'm sure Carly can give me a lift to—" She clutched her stomach and fell back against the couch, feeling another wave of sickness about to strike.

He poured hot water into a mug and brought it over to her. "Here, small sips." Sitting down next to her, he rubbed her back in a soothing circular motion.

"Thank you," she said, feeling the nausea starting to subside. She wondered how many more times she would be thanking him for one thing or another before the night was over.

"You should probably change out of that dress."

Or not. Ava glared at him. He wasn't seriously hitting on her, was he? How dare he take advantage of her in this state. Just how quickly could she run to the kitchen to grab a knife?

"No! No, I didn't mean ..." Thomas said, holding up his hand as though to stop her. "You can put away the daggers that are shooting out of your eyes. You just have some ..." He grimaced and pointed to Ava's chest where there were a few spots from her unexpected and unpleasant few minutes in the bathroom.

"Oh!" she exclaimed, mortified. Grabbing the sweatshirt and leggings she'd been wearing earlier, she ran back into the bathroom to change. She wouldn't have blamed Thomas for leaving after the way she'd treated him.

She entered the room again feeling refreshed and somewhat sober. Picking up her tea, she joined

Thomas on the couch. "Thanks again for this. It really is helping."

"I'm glad," he replied, smiling. "Right, well, if you're feeling better..." He stood up and smiled, before glancing toward the door.

"Thomas, I'm really embarrassed. I hardly ever get drunk like that. I mean, that's honestly never happened to me before, and ... well, you're an important client and all. I would never jeopardize that relationship or—"

"Not to worry. Cynthia doesn't need to know about any of this. Everything is just fine where that's concerned. I actually had a lovely evening getting to know you. These things happen to the best of us."

"Thank you. You've been so sweet to me all night. A perfect gentleman. You're really too good to be true." She stood up to give him a hug, but instead gave in to the urge to kiss him. His sensual, soft lips felt just as she imagined they would.

12

"You kissed him?" Carly shrieked as they worked on their portfolio sketches for Ms. Senaca's class. She'd reserved one of the private studios on campus to work on their project for finals. Ava's pieces were mostly done. She was really only there to add finishing touches and to keep Carly company.

"Yes," she responded with calmness in her voice, smudging the charcoal along the lines of Max's nude. She didn't consider it one of her best, yet she couldn't seem to put it down.

Carly stopped working on her project and looked over at Ava. "You kissed both of them?"

"Yes, that's what I told you. I kissed both of them."
She continued to work, not meeting Carly's stare. It
really wasn't that big of a deal.

"On the same day ... within a few hours of each
other."

"Well, technically, it was past midnight for
Thomas, so it wasn't the same day."

"Ava Haines! What has gotten into you? Now what
are you going to do?"

"What do you mean? There's nothing to do. Max
and I have already agreed that it won't happen again,
at least not while he's going to tutor me, and—"

"Hold on there! Did I hear you correctly? Did you
just say he's *tutoring* you?"

Carly stopped sketching, walked across the room,
and stood directly in front of Ava, demanding her full
attention.

She put down her charcoal and looked up. "Oh, did
I leave that part out?"

"Um, yeah! This story just keeps getting better and
better. All right, missy, explain." She pulled up a stool
and planted herself next to her friend, ready to hear all
of the juicy details.

Ava let out a dramatic sigh worthy of drama club
membership. "It's kind of a long story, but Suzanne
walked in on us ... you know, kissing. She got mad and
stormed out."

"I'll bet!" Carly laughed, clasping her hands
together. "From what you told me about that woman,

she probably hasn't ever been kissed, or laid for that matter. Now that I think about it, she could probably use a good—"

"Could I tell my story, please?" Ava interrupted. Sometimes talking to Carly was like talking to a thirteen-year-old boy. Not that she talked to many thirteen-year-old boys anymore, but between herself and her sisters, she'd crossed paths with quite a few. Their maturity level wasn't much different than her friend's at times.

"Go ahead," Carly encouraged, leaning forward and resting her forearms on her knees. "I'm not keeping you from telling your story. Tell away."

"As I was saying, it turns out that in addition to the nude modeling thing, Max is also a statistics geek, so he offered to tutor me."

She clutched her stomach and began laughing hysterically, nearly falling off her stool. "A match made in heaven," she said in between gasping for breaths. "Can I watch?"

"Watch what?" Ava went back to her drawing.

"Watch you squirm. Do you really think you're going to be able to concentrate with him in the room? If it was me, all I'd be thinking about is the kiss —and that." She pointed to the nude sketch. "Just how are you going to manage that?"

Ava pulled the drawing of Max off of her easel and replaced it with one from the lesson on facial features, which she'd originally wanted to work on during their studio time. She could feel her heart starting to race just thinking about Max's kiss. It was so passionate—raw. Yes, Thomas' kiss was wonderful, too, but Max's was ... she stopped to fan herself. *Easy, Ava.*

"I don't have a choice. I have to pass Statistics. Besides, he apologized and admitted it never should have happened. It was a mistake. He doesn't seem interested in anything beyond helping me."

"Too bad. Well, at least there's Thomas. What's his story? Habaneros, huh? That place is pretty intimate, and it isn't cheap, either. Guess flying photographers do pretty well these days."

Ava smiled to herself. Three hundred dollars for dinner and a ride home in a fancy sports car. Thank God she'd waited to get to her apartment before puking. She would have died of embarrassment right then and there had she gotten sick in his car. Not that any of that was important to her. She was more impressed that he'd made sure she was okay before he left, and that he hadn't tried to take advantage of her.

True to his word, he'd called to check up on her first thing this morning. He'd taken her to pick up her car, but she declined his breakfast offer, as her stomach had still been a little queasy. Instead, they'd made plans to have dinner. Of course, before that she had to get through a study session with Max. *Oh shit, Max!*

"What time is it?" Ava asked in a panic. She'd been so caught up in talking about the events of yesterday, she'd almost forgotten about her study session with her new tutor.

"Just about two o'clock, why?"

She threw her drawings into her portfolio. "I lost track of time. Max has a room reserved."

"Well, wham, bam, and thank you, ma'am!"

She shot Carly a look. "A room in Bauer Hall. Perhaps you've heard of it? It's that huge building also known as the *library*. We're going to study."

"Is that what you kids are calling it these days?"

"Whatever. I have to run. I'll see you tomorrow, okay?"

"Why tomorrow? You skipping pizza at the student center tonight?"

"I'm having dinner with Thomas."

"Again, huh? Well look at you. An afternoon romp with Max followed by a steamy date with Thomas. I've taught you well. Just make sure you keep yourself safe, young lady. There's a lot of scary stuff going around out there. Plus, you don't want any little Ava's running around, do you? You know what they say—*no glove, no love.*"

"Good-bye, Carly!" she shouted as she left the art studio shaking her head. *Yup. Thirteen-year-old boy.*

13

"I know, I'm late, I'm sorry!" Ava ran into the room panting. She dropped her Statistics book on the table with a thud.

"Don't worry about it," Max answered. He was already seated, his book and a pile of papers stacked neatly in front of him.

Damn he looks good, she thought to herself, wondering if she were now a sweaty, disheveled mess. Running across campus—even in the middle of December—was quite a workout. She slipped out of her jacket, slinging it over the back of an extra chair, and then checked her hands to make sure they were charcoal free. She hoped there was none smeared across her face. *Stop it, Ava. You're here to study.*

"Besides, I figured that the probability of you getting here on time was about forty-five percent." He looked at her and smiled, but she just sat there in silence with no response. "That's a little statistics humor." He cleared his throat and said, "Okay then. Why don't we get started?"

Ava pulled out what few notes she had. Normally she sat next to Suzanne to watch her go through problems, but decided it would be best if she sat across from Max. Even with their agreement to keep it all business, it was best to not to take any chances.

"So, what are we going to work on?" she asked.

"Well, I need to see what you know, and what you don't know, so I prepared a test for you to take." He pulled a sheet of paper out of his notebook and handed it to her.

"You're joking, right?"

"Um, no. I'm actually serious. How else will I know where to start?"

"Let's just assume I know nothing about this stuff and start from the beginning," She pushed the paper back to Max.

"That sounds fun, but we only have a few days. Just humor me, will you?" He pushed it back across the table.

"Oh fine." She looked down at the paper, trying to concentrate over the sound of a buzz coming from her phone. Ignoring it, she began working while Max looked through on his own textbook. Ten minutes later she was only on the second problem.

After Max declared time, he took the paper away from her, rubbing his temples, while examining her answers. Or lack of answers. The look on his face told her what she already knew.

"So three semesters of Basic Statistics and *nothing* clicked?"

Ava shook her head and shrugged.

"Okay, well here are some very basic rules and tricks. May I?" He pointed to the empty seat next to her.

She paused for a moment. "Sure." Certainly she could handle that for the sake of passing this stupid course.

He came around and sat next to her. As he pulled the chair in, his leg lightly brushed against hers, sending a tingle up her spine. She closed her eyes and desperately tried to re-focus.

"Do you understand?" he asked

"Could you explain that again, please?" she opened her eyes to see a piece of paper in front of her full of numbers and formulas. *Pay attention, Ava. Pay. Attention!*

He took out a fresh sheet and started over.

"Wait a minute, that's how you measure standard deviation? That actually makes sense. Why didn't anyone explain it like that before? Keep going."

Max continued to write down shortcuts to common formulas while her phone continued to buzz. Whoever it was could wait—she was too pumped up about her newfound knowledge.

"Don't you want to check that? It sounds like someone is trying to get in touch with you," he said. "You're doing really great. Let's take a break. I'll write up some problems for you from what we just went over."

She groaned, not wanting to lose momentum. Grabbing her phone, she walked over to the window. Might as well check. This time there were four text messages. The first two were from Carly with lewd comments about being alone in the room with Max. Then there onc from Tessa gushing about some boy she had a crush on in school who finally asked her out on a date, and the last one was from Thomas, apologizing for interrupting her studies, and letting her know he had to cancel their dinner date. She texted Thomas back that it was okay; then sent Tessa a quick congratulations. Carly's texts she ignored. She put her phone on silent and returned to the table, waiting while Max finished up. She felt absolutely giddy and didn't even care that Thomas had cancelled their plans. The important thing was that she understood statistics. *Finally.*

"Everything okay?" Max asked.

"Perfect," she answered, smiling. "You know, I have to admit, I didn't think this was going to work out at all. Well, that whole mess between us aside, I didn't think anyone would be able to teach me this stuff. I don't exactly have the best track record when it comes to understanding probabilities and all this other junk."

"So I heard."

"But I totally understood what you just taught me. And if I can understand that, then I just know I'll be able to understand the rest, too—or at least enough to pass. It all builds upon these basics, right?"

"Something like that."

"I haven't felt this positive about all of this in … well, in three semesters. Thank you!"

"Don't thank me yet," he said, placing a new sheet of problems in front of her. "Let's see if you can apply what you just learned to some of these."

A knock on the door interrupted them.

"Come in!" he yelled.

"Max?" A petite blonde with big blue eyes stepped just inside the door. Dressed in faded skintight jeans and an even tighter white sweater, Ava guessed her to be a size three. At least on the bottom— On the top, she was *much* bigger.

"Hi, you must be Megan." He got up from the table to shake her hand. "Ava, this is *my* statistics tutor, Megan Gillard. Megan, this is Ava Haines. I'm tutoring her in basic."

Getting to her feet, she felt the euphoria leave her body. This perfect specimen of brains and beauty was Max's tutor? "Nice to meet you," she lied.

"I'm afraid I'm going to have to kick you out of the room," he said, looking at Ava.

"What?"

"Sorry, it's my turn to be the student. Take this paper with you, and I'll meet you over there in about half an hour to check your answers." He pointed at an empty table near a window overlooking the parking area. "I know you'll do great. If you finish early, you can go over some of the material in the textbook in chapters one and two."

He handed her the sheet with an encouraging smile, before he pulled out a chair for Megan. Picking up her belongings, Ava walked out into the main room of the library. The door to the room she had shared with Max just moments before shut behind her with a quiet click. *Megan was just there to tutor him, right?*

14

Thirty minutes later, as promised, Megan and Max emerged from behind closed doors, giggling. Ava wished Suzanne was still around. Suzanne never giggled. *Never.* Max said good-bye to his tutor and headed over toward Ava's table. Tossing down his coat and books, he took the seat across from her this time, instead of next to her. She wondered what that meant, if anything. When did her brain become so damn analytical? What did it matter anyway? They were there to study. That's what they had agreed to.

"So she seemed nice," she said. *Ugh. Don't sound like a jealous girlfriend.*

She'd been sitting out here for thirty minutes staring at that door—and working on problems, but mostly staring at that door. As if *it* would tell her why she was thinking about Max so much when she should be thinking about Thomas—an awesome, handsome, sexy, *more mature* guy who actually liked her. Someone accomplished who worked in the arts, the field she hoped to have a career in someday. Not some egotistical numbers geek who liked to strut around nude.

"Who? Megan?" Max responded, looking at Ava strangely. "Well, she's helpful for sure. I was lucky to find her on such short notice."

"Yeah, lucky," she said through gritted teeth. *Focus, Ava.*

"So how did you do on your problems?"

She handed the paper over to him and waited while he looked them over.

"Well?" she asked. It was time to forget about the hot guy sitting across the table and get back to business. Was she really starting to understand all this number stuff—finally?

He smiled. "They're all correct."

"Seriously?"

He nodded. "You did it again."

"I actually feel like I'm getting the hang of this!"

He pulled out blank piece of paper, scribbled down another set of numbers and words, and slid it back over to her.

"What's this?" she questioned. "More?"

"Well, those were pretty basic. Let's see if you can take it one step further now. You don't have somewhere to be, do you? A hot date perhaps?" He winked and went back to his own work as she sighed.

"No," she replied, grabbing her pencil. Her hot date had, unfortunately, cancelled. She worked through each problem as best she could before handing them back over to Max.

He moved his pile of books to block her view, as he looked over her work. All she could see was the expression on his face—his crinkled nose, gritted teeth, and occasional grimace. He seemed to be taking an excruciatingly long time to examine her work.

"What's the hold up?" she finally asked, growing impatient. "Either I got them right or I didn't. And if I didn't, I'd like to know so I can work on fixing them. Time's ticking here. Less than a week until the exam."

He still didn't respond. He kept his eyes down and his brow furrowed, appearing to be deep in thought.

"Well, I guess that means I got them all wrong. Could I have it back so you can help now? Unless, of course, you have somewhere to be … a hot date perhaps?"

Max looked up, smirking. "Actually, you got them all right."

"What?" she shrieked. Then, remembering where she was, she lowered her voice to a whisper. "What?" she repeated.

"Yup. I have to admit, I can't quite believe it either. But you did. Every one of them. These weren't easy either. I even threw one in from my advanced class. I think if we just keep practicing these concepts you're going to be fine."

"Oh my God! Oh my God! I can't believe it!" Ava looked around the room, hoping her voice wasn't too loud again. She leaned in across the table to get closer to Max. "Thank you so much. You have no idea how grateful I am. Suzanne had been trying to teach me this stuff for like ever! Why didn't she show me these tricks?"

Smiling, Max raised his eyebrows.

"What do I owe you? Suzanne was getting twenty dollars an hour. We never talked about your rate or payment at all. Whatever it is, it's so worth it."

"Forget the money," he said, flashing his smile. "How about dinner tonight? Just you and me, somewhere quiet?"

Ava sat back in her chair. *There* was the Max she remembered from art class. Despite her earlier jealousy, she felt annoyed. Was this his plan all along? "What about what you said yesterday? *I can assure you that we will just study from now on.*"

"If it makes you feel better, we can bring the Statistics books with us." He grinned.

"I'd rather not, thanks."

"Fine then. Listen, I'm guessing you have to eat at some point, and you just said you wanted to pay me for the tutoring session. I'm just suggesting you pay me in food, that's all ... and maybe some company." He sat back in his chair and wrapped his fingers behind his head, looking smug.

She tilted her head to the side. "Oh, I see. You helped me, and now you want sex."

"Well, I really just wanted dinner, but if you're offering sex too—"

"No, I'm not. I was offering twenty dollars an hour."

"For sex?"

"No!" she exclaimed, feeling her face flame at the thought. The fact that she already knew what he looked like without clothes on didn't help.

Four people at the next table collectively "shushed" her.

"Sorry," she whispered to them.

"Come on, Ava. Let's just have dinner and talk about something other than statistics. We've both been working really hard. We deserve a little break. What do you say?"

She tapped her fingers on the table while she thought it over. Thomas cancelled, and the only food she had at her apartment was a loaf of stale bread that probably had fuzzy green things growing on it by now. That just left pizza with Carly at the cafeteria on campus. Her pickings were slim. "Oh, okay. Besides, the probability that I'll have sex with you is less than five percent anyway." She smirked and closed her books. "Do you want to meet at D'Angelos Café at six o'clock?"

"Nice choice. See you there."   He smiled before swinging his coat over one shoulder. "By the way, you know that means there's still a four point nine-nine percent chance," he added before disappearing amongst the stacks of books.

15

"So, flight school, huh? How long have you wanted to be a pilot?" Ava asked chewing a piece of grilled chicken from her salad. She would have preferred a pasta dish, but never ordered spaghetti on a first date. Not that this was a date or anything ... although she *would* be paying the bill, but only to thank Max for tutoring her. Even her thoughts rambled when she was nervous. She pushed the lettuce around on her plate as she waited for Max to respond.

"Ever since I was three. My parents took me to California to visit my grandparents. I'd never been on an airplane before, and thought it was the greatest machine I'd ever seen. A five-hour trip, and I couldn't sit still for any of it."

"Well, you *were* only three," she reminded him.

He ignored her and continued, "Aerodynamics is fascinating. One minute you're on the ground, the next you're in the air, able to travel to places in just hours that would otherwise take days or weeks—soaring through the clouds, thousands of miles off the ground, moving against gravity at incredible speeds. Completely defying nature. All it takes is something to be one thousandth of a millimeter off, and that plane is nose-diving down. There's no chance of survival when that happens."

Ava jumped when he crashed his hands together, to simulate thc poor plane's demise.

"I gotta say, you're really not making it sound all that appealing."

"Oh, I'm just messing with you. It's actually the safest form of travel. Don't you like to fly?"

"I've never been."

"You're kidding. Really? Never? Wow!" He shook his head, then laughed when he realized she was serious.

What the hell was so funny? She took another bite of her salad, trying to decide if she was insulted or not. She chose to brush it off and change the subject. "So nude modeling—you know there *are* other ways to make money."

He looked up her, still smiling. "Maybe, but the money was good. Besides, I had something nice to look at also."

Ava felt the heat rushing to her face and wished they were still talking about flying. She once again pushed her lettuce around her plate, pretending to be more interested in her salad than her dinner companion.

"What about you? A dual degree in art and business is pretty ambitious. What do you plan to do with that?" He spun a few strands of spaghetti around his fork and popped it in his mouth, spaghetti she had wanted to order for herself.

"Short term, I'm hoping that the art gallery where I'm interning will offer me a job after graduation. A paying job that is."

"And long-term?" Max gazed across the table at her. He seemed genuinely interested in what she had to say.

"Long-term, I'd like to have an art gallery of my own someday."

He continued to sit there staring at her. Maybe it wasn't interest. Maybe it was boredom.

"Sounds dumb, right?" *Great*, she thought. *He's probably trying to think up some excuse now why he has to cut dinner short.*

"No, not at all." He put an elbow on the table and rested his chin on his hands "I think it sounds perfect."

"Thanks." She smiled at his response. Even if he didn't mean it, he looked and sounded so sincere.

"There's another reason I chose to be a nude model, you know."

"You mean besides wanting to show the world your stunning good looks?" Ava glanced at her empty wine glass and wondered if maybe that second round was too much—especially after the drinking disaster she'd just had with Thomas.

"Thanks ... I think," he answered. "Actually, I'm a huge art fan myself. My trip to California was only the first of many I took as a child. My parents were big into culture. We traveled the world and stopped at every museum along the way. The art museums were always my favorite."

Tilting her head, Ava regarded Max, wondering if his story was true. *Art Museums*? Was he for real, or was this just some ploy to get her more interested in him? It was hard to keep the sarcasm from her voice when she asked, "Oh really? And which one was your favorite?"

"Well, I've been to so many—the Louvre in Paris, the National Gallery in London ... then there was the Van Gogh Museum in Amsterdam, the Vatican Museum in Rome, and of course our own Metropolitan Museum of Art in New York City."

She sat back in her seat, arms crossed, unimpressed. Okay, so he knew the names of the biggest art museums around the world. Big deal. Most people could rattle off those. He still didn't answer the question. "So they're all your favorite?"

"They're all amazing. But my favorite? That belongs to the Musée de l'Orangerie."

"In Paris," Ava added, now more intrigued than ever by this person sitting across from her. "Interesting choice."

Max leaned across the table, and she swore she saw a sparkle in his eye as he began to talk ... well, gush was more like it. "Monet's paintings are spectacular ... and enormous, like nothing you will see in any of his other pieces. The rooms where the *Water Lilies* are housed are oval shaped, and the paintings are made up of massive panels set around them. They completely surround you. It's amazing. Everywhere you look in the room, you are pulled into his scenery. It's a masterpiece of pure beauty and tranquility. I could sit there for hours."

With eyes-wide, she hung on his every word, feeling her breathing beginning to slow.

He gazed off in the distance, as though seeing everything he was describing. "You really got a sense of the emotion Monet must have been feeling as he painted his gardens. The way he captured the change in the natural light was just—" He shuddered slightly and shook his head, as if trying to bring himself back into the present. "Oh, I must sound like a complete dork talking like that about a bunch of paintings —of flowers no less."

Ava smiled. Her need to be on guard around him was easing up. Even if he was making it all up, he'd gone to a lot of trouble to learn about her favorite paintings, by her favorite artist, in her favorite museum. Not that she'd ever been there, but given the choice to visit just one museum in the entire world, she would choose that one hands down.

"Not at all, it's always been a dream of mine to go there."

"I hope one day you can," he replied, glancing around the restaurant as if unsure of what to say next. "So, we should probably get going. I'm meeting Megan early in the morning for tutoring."

"Oh." Just the mention of her name made Ava cringe. She tried to shake off the negative feelings. He was there with her tonight, not Megan. Besides, she was just a tutor. Of course, Max was just Ava's tutor, too. Did she want more? *No. Yes.* After that conversation they just had, maybe. "I'm sorry. I've been so focused on my own exam. I tend to forget you're having trouble as well. You've spent so much time helping me. I really appreciate it."

He signaled for the check when the waitress walked by. "It's fine. I'm happy to do it. I have my afternoon free tomorrow. Do you want to get in some more study time?"

"That would be great. Thanks," she said, reaching out for the check the waitress was holding.

Max snatched it before her fingers even grazed the paper.

"Hey! I'm supposed to pay, remember? To thank you for tutoring?"

"You can get the next one," he told her.

"So there's going to be a next one?" she asked playfully.

He waved the check in front of her face and smiled. "There is now, but only if you get all of your problems right tomorrow."

"Oh, I'm going to get them right, don't you worry. And I'm going to pay for dinner, too. Got it?"

"Yes, ma'am. You sure are cute when you're bossy, did you know that? Come on. I'll walk you home."

16

Ava excused herself to use the restroom before they left. The walk back to her apartment was only a few blocks, however she needed a couple of minutes to regroup and get advice. She considered contacting Carly, but knew that would probably only end in disaster. Instead, she called her sister.

"Holly? Can you hear me?" she asked when she heard the familiar voice pick up. She tried to keep her voice down, not knowing if anyone else was in the bathroom. D'Angelos Café was a popular place to eat among Wolfenson students.

"Ava? What's up? I can barely hear you. Is everything okay?"

"I'm in the restroom, and I only have a few minutes. I'm on a date."

"With that Thomas guy?" Holly asked.

"No, I'm with Max."

"What happened to Thomas? I thought you were having dinner together tonight? Wait. Who's Max?"

Ava sighed and started to explain. "Okay, so Thomas and I were supposed to have a date tonight, but he cancelled. Max is the guy I told you about from art class. You know, the model? It's a long story, but he's now tutoring me in statistics."

"You know this isn't making much sense, right?"

"I don't really have time to explain right now, except we kissed—Max and me. Well Thomas and I kissed, too, but this is about Max. Anyway, we said it shouldn't have happened – the kiss, I mean, and now he's tutoring me, and he's about to walk me home."

"From tutoring?"

"No, from our date. At least I think it's a date. I offered to buy him dinner to thank him because he wouldn't let me give him money. Except he grabbed the check and wound up paying it."

"Geez, Av, you really took that *I'm going to stay man-free so I can focus on finals* advice to heart, didn't you?" her sister teased.

"Hol, I need advice, not mocking. I like both of them, Thomas and Max. What should I do?"

"Do what you tell me to do ... follow your heart, and don't get caught. Speaking of, I gotta go. There's this guy, Jared, and he's super cute. My roommate knows his roommate, and she's introducing us tonight. Wish me luck."

"Thanks—and good luck."

Ava hung up the phone, reapplied her lipstick, checked her hair, and returned to the table where Max was patiently waiting.

"Ready?"

She nodded.

They walked closely side by side, without holding hands, despite Ava's hope that they would.

The night was chilly, but not freezing cold, a rarity for December, a month generally filled with frigid temperatures. Ava could comfortably keep her hands out of her pockets ... just in case he reached for her. The sounds of cars driving by, and college students chatting as they passed, were barely noticeable—she was thinking only about the kiss to come.

Would it come? After all, they *had* kissed before, even though it had been unexpected, at least for her. True, Max said it shouldn't have happened and had promised to keep their relationship on a strictly professional level. But things were different now, weren't they? Was this a date, or was Ava reading too much into it?

And what about Thomas? Did she owe him some sort of loyalty? They'd only had one date, but had never discussed the status of their relationship, even if they had a relationship. Besides, if Thomas was so important to her, why couldn't she stop thinking about Max? She was certain she already knew the answer to that question.

"Are you okay?" he asked.

She realized they'd come to a stop – right outside of her apartment. *Had she ignored Max all the way home?*

"Hmm? I'm fine, why?"

"You seem so quiet. I think I lost you about half a block into the walk back."

Ava stared at the sky. Moonlight shone down on the two of them like a spotlight, cancelling out everything else around them as stars danced above.

"No, it's just such a nice night, that's all. Thanks for dinner and for the tutoring again. I really appreciate it. Of course, I still owe you for that, you know. Oh, and good luck with your studies tomorrow. I guess I'll see you in the afternoon? And thanks also for walking me home. I suppose I'll be going inside now." Ava hated this part. She always felt so self-conscious and rambled way too much. She wished Max would kiss her already. She pretended to be searching for her keys in her purse, even though she knew they were in her coat pocket.

"So," he began, "I know we kind of got off to a weird start with you seeing me naked, and me shoving you up against a wall to kiss you, and all."

"Yeah, that was a bit out of the ordinary and admittedly awkward," she agreed.

"Do you think we could start over?"

She smiled and nodded. "I'd like that." She was already feeling more relaxed.

"Hi, I'm Max Wallis. I'm a senior at Wolfenson College where I tutor statistics. It's nice to meet you." He stuck out his hand.

Ava giggled, replying, "It's very nice to meet you, Max Wallis, I'm Ava Haines. I'm also a senior at Wolfenson, and I happen to need a statistics tutor. I heard you're very good." She took his hand and shook it.

He gently pulled Ava toward him and leaned in for a kiss ... a soft, lingering kiss that she felt to her toes. While so different than their first encounter, there was no mistaking that she felt the same weakness in her knees.

He pulled away slowly, whispering in her ear, "I'd be happy to tutor you. Would tomorrow afternoon work? Two o'clock, usual spot?"

"Definitely," she whispered back, barely able to recover.

17

"No, Carly. We've already been through this. You can't come with me. It's a tutoring session."

Carly pulled a low cut blouse out of Ava's closet and handed it to her friend to wear.

"No," she said, hanging it back up, before finding and putting on a casual sweater. "I repeat—it's a tutoring session."

"Do you always do your hair like that for *tutoring?*"

"You don't want me to look like a complete slob, do you?"

"Well, can I at least tell you *I told you so?*"

Ava paused in the middle of zipping a boot. "What did you *tell me*?"

"I told you that you two would wind up together," Carly reminded her.

"I have no recollection of you ever saying that. I only recall you stating he was hot ... so yes, I agree, he's hot." Ava smiled. "*Totally hot.*"

"And I told you he was into you, remember?"

"Maybe." She grinned. Oh yes, Carly had said that. Ava remembered it clearly, and she'd been right. After the kiss last night, there was no doubt that Max was into her. The feeling was mutual.

"So, um, what are you going to do about Thomas?"

"I don't know." She hadn't given him much thought since last night. She guessed she'd just have to be honest about it. It was probably a good idea to get their relationship back on a business track anyway with his exhibit coming up so soon. "I'll figure something out. Right now, I need to concentrate on studying."

Carly laughed. "Studying ... right. This I have to see."

"I told you, you're not coming along."

"Last I heard, the library's a public place. If I want to sit and watch from across the room, you can't stop me."

"Carly!"

"Oh, please. It's not like you two are going to be able to do anything good there anyway. Don't worry.

I've no intention of spying on you. I don't want to break my perfect record."

Ava was afraid to ask, but she had to know. "Record for what?"

"I'm determined to be the first person to graduate Wolfenson without ever stepping foot in the library." She smiled proudly. "Anyway, I have to run, I've got studio time booked. You'll text me all the under the table details later, right?"

She looked at her friend and rolled her eyes.

"So the library ... that's the big building in the center of campus with the dome?" Carly asked winking as she walked out of the apartment.

Ava waited for the door to close before she fixed her hair one more time.

She looked at the clock. Two fifteen. Max had said two o'clock, hadn't he? She supposed she was a tad bit distracted last night. Maybe he'd said three, or perhaps he'd meant the study room and not the table where they'd worked before. Usual spot could mean either now that she thought about it. She got up to look inside of the private room. Another group sat in there studying.

"Ava?" When she returned, a guy she didn't recognize was standing next to the table where she'd been sitting.

"Yes?"

He was sort of non-descript looking—skinny, brown hair, glasses, wearing a Wolfenson sweatshirt. He seemed like your average college student. She probably did know him, and she felt bad that she couldn't remember.

He put a stack of books down on the table and stuck out his hand. "I'm Barry Templin. Max sent me. He apologizes, but he's not going to be able to make it. He thought I could help you study today instead."

She rubbed her forehead. Surely she misunderstood. "Not going to make it? Are you sure? Last night he said he'd meet me here."

Barry nodded. "Yes, he called me this morning and asked if I could take over as your tutor. We met earlier so he could show me where you and he left off. He asked me to give you this." He handed Ava a sealed envelope with her name on it. "He also told me he'd be paying for your sessions."

She took the envelope out of his hand. "Forgive me. I just … I'm afraid I don't understand. Are you telling me that Max won't be tutoring me at all—ever?"

"I don't know about ever," he responded, "but not through these final exams. At least that's what it sounded like to me. Don't worry. I'm a math major. I've been tutoring statistics students for quite a while now. I'll get you through this exam without any problems."

Suddenly, the room felt too warm to breathe. Like the air had grown heavy. Or maybe it was her heart. After last night, after realizing how much she liked him, Max wasn't coming. Ever, from the sounds of it. Feeling a little sick to her stomach, she sank into one of the chairs at the table.

"Thanks. But—um— would it be okay if we skipped today? I—think I'm coming down with something." *Not tutoring me anymore?*

"Sure, no problem." He scribbled his name and number on a sheet of paper and handed it to her. "Just give me a call when you're ready to schedule something. It was nice to meet you."

"Nice to meet you, too, and thanks." She watched as he collected his books and walked off before opening the letter from Max. Her hands trembled as she pulled the paper out of the envelope.

Dear Ava,

I know you probably hate me right now, and I don't blame you. I'm pretty upset with myself actually. I made a promise to you when I agreed to be your tutor that we would keep everything professional, and I totally crossed that line last night—the same way I crossed it the day Suzanne walked in on us. As your mentor, I had a responsibility to you, and I failed. I know how important passing this class is to you, and I promise I won't distract you from that again. Good luck. Barry is a great tutor. I know with his help you'll have no trouble passing the exam.

Max

Ava read the letter twice. *Coward.* He had no problem flirting with and kissing her last night. Why the sudden change? Barry said he contacted him this morning. Didn't Max say he had an early meeting with Megan? Did *she* have something to do with his sudden change of heart?

Her hurt turned to anger, as she sat there wondering what had changed. *How dare he! How dare he not have the guts to tell her to her face! How dare he treat last night as a date! How dare he kiss her like that* ... she wiped the tear as it rolled down her cheek.

She looked at the text message she'd received earlier.

So sorry about last night. Please say you'll let me make it up to you tonight. Dinner at La Trattoria? - Thomas

Ava read the letter one more time, blinking back any remaining tears. Looking back down at her phone, she typed:

Sounds perfect.

18

"Holly! Did you tell Tessa that I'm dating two guys at once?" Ava demanded the moment she heard her sister's voice on the other end of the phone. "She's sixteen for God's sake. She looks up to us … me in particular. Dad would kill her if he caught her running around like that. Hell, he'd kill me, too." As the oldest of the Haines children, she felt a responsibility—particularly to Tessa, who was still in high school, to set a good example. Leave it to Holly to open her big mouth. Of course, her youngest sister thought it was the coolest thing ever, judging by the text Ava received when returning from the library.

Way to work it, sis! Two guys in one weekend? Me and Hol want to know your secret.

"Well, it's true. You did go out with two different guys this weekend. So who's the lucky one tonight?" Holly teased.

"Thomas," she mumbled. "But, I'm not dating two guys anymore. It's just Thomas." Her heart ached as she said the words. *Damn him.*

"Why, what happened?"

Ava really didn't want to relive the entire experience, but she knew her sister wouldn't let up until she explained.

"Wow, that's rough," she said after hearing the entire sordid story. "But at least you have a fall back guy. I always say you need a fall back guy. That's what I was trying to explain to Tessa. See? You just proved my point."

"Do me a favor, and leave my love life out of your discussions with her, okay? In fact, let's leave my love life out of discussions all together. Let's talk about you. Wasn't there some guy you were chasing? What happened with him?"

"Jared? He's really cute, but he doesn't seem interested. At least not yet. I'm still working on him, though." Ava could see Holly's smile through the phone. She knew her so well she could almost see the wheels turning in her head, the plots and plans she was coming up with. This poor Jared guy didn't stand a chance against Holly Haines if she'd made up her mind that she wanted him.

"I'm sure you'll figure out a way. But, I've got to go get ready for my date. Be good, you hear me?"

"Always."

"I think I'll pass on the alcohol tonight," Ava said when Thomas offered her a look at the wine menu.

He laughed. "Can't really say I blame you. So how's the studying coming along?"

"It's good, I guess. You wouldn't happen to know anything about statistics, would you?"

"Wretched subject," he replied. "Why would you torture yourself with that rubbish?"

"It's not by choice, trust me. It's required. I'm embarrassed to even tell you how many times I've already attempted to pass it. Luckily, I think I've finally got it this time. Max was able to—" Ava stopped herself short. Just saying his name out loud hurt, and it didn't make any sense. She barely knew the guy. It shouldn't matter that he didn't want to see her anymore—except it did.

"Max was able to? What?"

"Oh, nothing. He was my tutor. I was just going to say I think I understand most of the concepts this time. At least I think I understand enough to pass.

That's all that matters, really. I'm past the point of trying to get a good grade. All I want is to be done with it already."

The waitress brought over Thomas' glass of wine and Ava's water.

"Well, here's to passing then," he stated, raising his drink.

"Yes, to passing. And to *not* talking about statistics anymore tonight," she added, lightly tapping Thomas' glass.

"So I spent the day at the gallery with Cynthia," he said, changing the subject right on cue.

"How'd it go? I missed being there yesterday."

"We seem to have almost everything in order to open on Friday. There are so many little details to see to between now and then. Well, look who I'm telling. Of course you know all about that. I don't think artists really appreciate how much behind the scenes work goes into each one of these events. Cynthia spent hours showing me everything from menu items to the colors you and she chose for the bloody tablecloths. It was exhausting."

Ava shrugged. "All the planning is part of the fun for me."

"Well, I'm just glad I'm the one behind the camera most of the time. I could never do the spectacular job that you do. I guess we make a good team. Speaking of, I'd love to take some photos of you one day. Your face has such beautiful lines."

"Oh," she replied, putting her hands to her cheeks. She could feel the heat radiating off of them. "Yes, I would like that. I've never had professional photos taken. Maybe after the opening."

"It's a date then," Thomas announced, smiling. "This is turning out to be quite an exhilarating week for me! It's been ages since I've had a big opening like this. In fact, I don't know who's more excited for Friday night, Cynthia or me," he laughed.

"Don't forget me. I'm excited, too, you know."

"I could never forget you, sweetheart," he cooed, his eyes tender as he gazed at her.

Except for her parents, no one had ever called her sweetheart before. She liked how it sounded. She only wished—

Dinner with Thomas was so different than it had been the night before with Max. She'd been playful and flirty with him. Here she felt more regal, refined, and chic. Did she prefer one style to the other? It didn't matter. *There was no her and Max anymore. Not that there ever had been. Just enjoy the here and now, Ava.*

"I'm sorry, what were you saying?"

Thomas laughed. "I can see you still have your studies on your mind. I remember those days. I was saying that Cynthia talked about you non-stop. I think it's safe to say that once your internship is over, she'll be keeping you on full-time. If that's what you're interested in, of course."

"Really, do you think so?" Her eyes widened. She knew Cynthia was considering the possibility, but no offers had been made yet. She was glad to hear that her boss was so pleased with her work.

He reached across the table, taking her hands in his own. "Yes, in fact, Cynthia and I go way back. If she's not already convinced, I can see to it that she will be."

Ava smiled. Seemed this day was turning out to be a good one after all.

19

"Forget about him, Ava. He was only eye-candy. Totally not worth your time."

Sitting across from her friend in the library, Ava tried to figure out three things— One, why was Carly even in the library. Wasn't she trying to set some sort of world record? Two, why she suddenly was telling Ava to forget about Max after spending the last week trying to convince her he was perfect for her. And three, why she herself couldn't stop looking at the table across the room where Max sat studying with Megan.

She was trying to forget about him, but it wasn't easy. Especially when he was in the same room, and

Carly couldn't seem to stop talking about him. Of course, she could always get up and move, but why should she? She was here first. Not that moving would help. He'd still be etched in her brain.

She'd purposely sat at a table on the fifth floor, figuring he wouldn't be here. He normally used the third floor. When he showed up with Megan, Ava ducked behind a stack of books hiding out of sight until he'd settled at his table with his back to her. She was pretty sure he had no idea she was sitting across the room behind him.

"Anyway," Carly continued, "you've got Thomas." She held out her hands like a scale, palms up, weighing each of the men Ava had encountered over the past few days. "Good-looking, yet immature college guy who has to pose nude to make money and can't make up his mind about what he wants, or older, yet established and sophisticated artist who happens to be wealthy and oh yeah, he's got that sexy accent, too." Carly raised her palm—the one representing Thomas— above her head, while dropping the other one—the one signifying Max—as low as she could reach. "Seems to me you got the better end of the deal."

Ava nodded. "Thomas is pretty awesome. I could listen to him talk for hours, and not just because of his accent. He's got so many great stories from his career, and life in general, that we never run out of conversational topics. I don't think I've ever met anybody so accomplished. Yesterday, after I finished up my last art project, he took me out to Carver's for lunch. You know that steakhouse over on Fitz Street?"

"You're kidding," Carly said, her jaw dropping in surprise. "I've never been there. In fact, other than you, I've never even known anyone who's been there. Isn't the chef from one of those celebrity cooking shows? I thought there was like a year's waiting list to get in there."

"There is, and yes, his name is Georges Apollo. Apparently, Thomas is friends with the guy. He has his number in the contacts on his cell the same way I have yours. Can you imagine? I even got to meet him yesterday."

"Get out!" Carly exclaimed, then covered her mouth before whispering, "Sorry," to the people at the tables directly around them.

"It's true." She grinned, knowing most of the people on campus – the professors included – would be green with envy. "I couldn't believe it myself. Of course, Thomas didn't warn me ahead of time. He only texted me and asked if I wanted to take a study break to grab some lunch, so I had paint all over me when he came to pick me up. I figured he meant a burger at The Spot, you know? Thankfully, it was dark in the dining room."

"You're living the dream, Ava."

"I don't know about that. I'm certainly eating well, that's for sure."

"And?" Carly asked, chin resting on her hand, a glazed look in her eye.

"And what?"

"And what about the romance part?"

"I guess it's fine. He's a really good kisser." Ava smiled. *He was a really good kisser.*

"That's it? That's all I get? *He's a really good kisser?*"

"Well, there hasn't been anything more than that to tell. I don't know. I haven't really felt all that much in the way of sparks flying past kissing. He seemed like he wanted more yesterday when he dropped me off, but I made an excuse that I had to get back to studying. Well, it wasn't an excuse, exactly. I *did* have to study. My Statistics test is tomorrow, you know. But I'm just not feeling it with him. I hope he doesn't think I'm taking advantage of him. I mean, I do really like him. He's a great guy, super interesting to talk to and all. I'm just not sure I'm there yet— sexually." Ava glanced over to Max's table again. Megan was now sitting much closer to him. She tried to shake off the pangs of jealousy racing through her mind before looking back at Carly.

"You just need more time. Be patient. Not everyone has that instant chemistry. They actually say the best relationships are ones where you start out as friends first."

"When did you become such an expert on romance?"

"I just know, that's all. He really likes you, I can tell."

"You said that about Max, too." Ava glanced at his table again. She wished she could keep herself from looking. They were laughing now. What was so funny about statistics? Nothing. They obviously weren't studying. *Stop it, Ava. It's not your concern.* He turned his head mid-laugh and caught her eye across the room. He quickly looked away.

"Well, he did like you. It's not my fault he wound up being a major ass. Anyway, I told you to forget about him. So do you have plans with Thomas tonight?" Carly asked.

"No. I've got my exam tomorrow, and then the exhibit."

"Busy day."

"You're telling me. Statistics is first thing in the morning. Right after that I've got a meeting with Cynthia and Thomas. Next I have to get the gallery ready, then I have to get myself ready, and after that of course, is the big event. Somewhere in between, I need to find time for a nap."

"Sleep the next day," Carly said. "Besides, you'll be too ramped up on adrenaline to be tired."

"Probably." She knew that's exactly how it would be. Openings always thrilled her, and she would be too excited to sit still, much less sleep.

"Then you get an entire week alone here with Thomas while the rest of campus goes home for the holidays, including me."

"Are you coming tomorrow night?"

"Of course. Your openings are the best party in town. I do have to leave first thing the next day though. You better promise to text me if anything *interesting* happens while I'm gone."

Ava rolled her eyes and smiled. She was definitely going to miss Carly over the break.

20

Thomas brushed Ava's lips lightly as she got out of her car. He'd been waiting for her to arrive before going inside for their meeting. She glanced around him to scan the parking lot, wanting to make sure Cynthia was safely inside the gallery. With the coast seemingly clear, she wrapped her arms around him, savoring the taste of his tongue and lips, while taking in the clean smell of his skin. She hadn't lied to Carly—she enjoyed kissing him immensely.

"Thank you for the flowers," she said as she pulled away, smiling. "You didn't have to."

Just as Ava had been getting ready to leave her apartment for her Statistics final earlier, a dozen red roses arrived. The card wished her good luck on her exam and was signed: "Love, Thomas."

"I know I didn't," he replied, tracing her lips with his fingers. "I wanted to. How'd it go?"

"Good," she smiled. She couldn't have quashed the excitement in her voice for the world. "I really think I passed. In fact, I'm sure of it!"

He kissed her again, holding her in his arms even tighter than he had before. "Then tonight we'll have two things to celebrate!"

"No. Tonight is all about you. We can celebrate my exam when I find out my grade. I don't want to jinx it."

"Sounds like a plan. We should go inside before Cynthia comes out looking for us."

They held hands as they crossed the parking lot and walked along the side of the gallery. The moment they were within range of the front windows, they separated—turning instantly into business acquaintances.

"Look who I ran into outside," Thomas said enthusiastically, giving Cynthia a kiss on each cheek before patting Ava's shoulder as if he were presenting a prize.

"Fabulous! Are you all done with schoolwork now, dear?" her boss asked.

"Yes, I had my last final this morning."

"Perfect!" She clapped her hands together. "We've got a lot of work ahead of us. There are only a few hours until the opening, and I still feel like there's so much to do. To be honest, I'm feeling a bit overwhelmed, and those other interns have been useless. They've all left to go home for winter break." She rolled her eyes. "I've missed having you here."

"Thank you, but, the gallery looks great."

"Well that's because Cynthia incorporated so many of your ideas," Thomas said, but quickly added, "Of course, you're very fortunate to have such a great talent to mentor you." Putting an arm around Cynthia, he kissed her on the cheek.

"Oh, now stop it." She swatted Thomas away, giggling. "Are you sure I can't convince you to stay over the holidays, Ava?"

"I'm sorry. I'm afraid if I don't go home, my family—my sisters in particular—will come hunt me down and drag me back to Forest Hills. We're all very close."

"You're lucky. I don't have any siblings, and what's left of my family isn't nearby at all. It's going to be lonely here. And Thomas, you'll be off to your next exhibit soon. I really am thrilled that you chose my gallery to start off your tour. It's a shame we only get to see each other once every ten years. Let's try to do something about that, shall we?"

Ava glanced over to him, registering what her boss had just said. It never occurred to her that he didn't live locally. The way he'd always talked made it sound like this was his home. Even after asking Ava where she was from, he'd never once mentioned that he lived somewhere else.

"You're leaving?" she asked.

"Yes," Thomas responded calmly, as if he were speaking to an acquaintance and not to someone he had been intimate with just moments ago. "I live in the Pacific Northwest, in British Columbia. It's quite beautiful there—a photographer's paradise. Maybe one day you can come out to visit with your family. Of course, I won't be returning there right away. After I leave here, I'll be visiting the various other galleries who are kind enough to display my work. I'll make my way across the country over the next six months, back toward my home."

"Oh," she murmured, trying not to sound disappointed or surprised. *British Columbia?* That wasn't even in the same country! "That sounds lovely. I didn't realize you lived so far away." She then turned to Cynthia, suddenly feeling as if all the walls were closing in on her. "Would you excuse me for a moment? I'm not sure I locked my car."

She left the gallery without waiting for her response, and leaned against the side of the building, trying to steady her breathing. *It's okay. There were no sparks, remember? But there could have been. Even Carly said all the best relationships started out as friendships first. And he sure acted like he felt sparks. What was that all about? Whatever. It didn't matter now. Nice work, Ava, You're oh-for-two. Breathe. No big deal. He's a client anyway. It's better this way. He's just a client. A client who didn't give you sparks. Well, maybe some sparks, but not enough. Breathe. Just a client ... a client you will never see again after this week.*

She collected herself and walked back inside—feeling Thomas' eyes following her every move.

"Is everything okay?" Cynthia asked, an odd look on her face.

"Hmm?" Ava replied. "Oh, yes. Everything is fine. I did actually forget to lock my car. It's all set now. Shall we get to work?"

21

"Well now, aren't you looking hot!" Carly whistled as she circled Ava. "Nobody's going to be noticing Thomas' photos tonight. They're going to be too busy checking you out."

"Too much?" she asked, adjusting the straps on the dress Carly let her borrow. Specifically the tight black one that seemed to be a little light on fabric. Ava wasn't used to having so much skin showing. "Or should I say, too little?" she added, twisting around to see herself in the mirror.

"Nope, it's perfect."

"How do you sit in this thing?" she asked, trying to slip into the matching black heels. There didn't seem to be a graceful way to stoop down without showing the world all she had to offer. The dress was so tight she was afraid it might tear if she made any sudden moves.

"You don't. You'll be standing all evening. That is, until you're ready to take it off … as in *take it off.*" Carly did an imitation of a strip tease wiggle as she winked at Ava.

"The only time I'll be taking this off is to go to sleep. As in *go to sleep.* Thomas and I are through."

"What? When? How? I can't keep up with you. Explain. Now."

Ava filled her friend in on everything that had happened. The flowers and the card. The *love, Thomas.* The kiss in the parking lot. And the fact that he lived the width of a continent away.

"So what?" Carly asked. "Lots of people have long distance relationships."

"You don't get it," she said as she applied her makeup. She rarely wore bright red lipstick, but the dress demanded it. "He never had an interest in a long distance relationship. If he had, he would have told me right at the beginning that he didn't live here. Not once did he mention it. In fact, even after he told me where he lived, he didn't seem to care whether he saw me again or not. His exact words were, 'Maybe one day you can come out to visit with your family.' A *maybe,* Carly, not a *you must,* but a *maybe*—and with my family no less."

"Ooh, ouch."

"He only had an interest in a week long fling. You know ... a girl in every port kind of thing? He knew exactly what he was doing. Well, no thanks. He can find someone else to cozy up with until he leaves."

"So what's with the dress, then? I just assumed it was for Thomas. Oh, I get it! It's a screw you dress." She nodded in approval and smiled. "Nice touch."

"What are you talking about? I just want to look nice tonight. It's a big event."

"No, no, no. I know exactly what this is. This is a dress that says '*you're an asshole for treating me this way ... look at what you could have had*' dress. It's cool. I would have done the same thing. It totally works—especially with the lipstick. Anyway, maybe there'll be some other hot guy tonight who will take one look at you in that getup and fall head over heels."

Ava sighed. "No more guys. I'm finished. I just want to get through this week so I can go home for the holidays." Her heart had fallen for too many guys in too few days as it was. She wasn't sure it could take another beating. At least not for a while. "Are you ready? I don't want to be late."

Carly adjusted her own skintight dress one more time, giving her mirrored reflection a nod of approval, before turning to Ava, "Yup, let's go."

The girls arrived at the gallery with ten minutes to spare. Ava had hoped to get there a little earlier, but Cynthia had left her very little time to get ready, working her hard the entire afternoon. Once the meeting with Thomas ended, he stuck around briefly to try to speak to her, but she just ignored him until he finally got the hint and left. After that, her boss put her in charge of decorations and adding final touches to the set up. *Cynthia's* afternoon, on the other hand, consisted of appointments at the spa with her hair and makeup people.

"Ava, dear," Cynthia said, taking hold of her hands, excitement lighting her eyes. "The gallery looks beautiful. You've really outdone yourself this time. Tonight is going to be a smashing success, I can feel it."

As she looked around, she couldn't help but agree. She was incredibly proud of her efforts. The gallery had looked wonderful when she left to go back to her apartment to get dressed, but was even more elegant now that the sun had set. Without the brightness of the outside sunshine streaming in through the windows, the strategically placed spotlights emphasized the strengths of each photo perfectly. She'd worked hard to make sure each photograph was displayed and grouped in such a manner as to prominently display its maximum artistic beauty. To lend a festive air, silver balloons, confetti, and streamers had been scattered here and there to help celebrate opening night.

Bowls of votive candles were set on tables in each of the rooms, casting their glow on elegantly placed business cards and brochures in case anyone wanted to know more about their featured artist. A trio of musicians sat in the corner playing soft classical music, and men and women dressed in black and white catering attire were already in position with trays of hors d'oeuvres and champagne, waiting for the guests to arrive.

Her feelings for Thomas were irrelevant. The gallery's reputation was at stake, as was her career. Her position and integrity required her to do the best possible job she knew how, and she'd done exactly that.

Cynthia was absolutely glowing as she sashayed across the floor in a silver gown that matched the balloons. "This is it, Ava! Everything is ready to go, and it's just about time to open." She peered out the window, as if expecting to see mobs of people waiting outside. "Wonderful, here comes Thomas now."

Just as he approached, Ava took a deep breath and unlocked the door. He paused as he took in her appearance; it was as if she took his breath away for a brief moment.

"Ava—" he began.

"Oh, Thomas!" Cynthia gushed, hurrying up to him and kissing him on each cheek. "Isn't this just beautiful? My fabulous intern worked tirelessly all afternoon."

"Yes, just stunning," he replied, not taking his eyes off Ava.

"Come," she ordered, whisking Thomas away. "I want to give you the grand tour. The caterer and bartender are set up in the alcove, and over here ..."

Ava could hear Cynthia's voice trail off as she guided him toward the back of the gallery and into the next room.

"Told you," Carly whispered, grabbing a glass of champagne from one of the trays getting ready to be passed around.

Her lips curved in a satisfactory grin as she welcomed the first guests to arrive for the opening.

22

Within minutes, the gallery filled with people chattering, laughing, and complimenting Thomas' photography as they walked through, sipping champagne and nibbling appetizers. Ava stood to the side, ready to answer any questions, of course, but mostly she was enjoying the moment.

She watched as Cynthia worked the room, effortlessly gliding from one guest to the next, pointing to whichever of Thomas' photos they happened to be standing in front of. She recited stories of each picturesque scene, whether or not they were true, in order to sell the lovely works of art. After all, at the end of the day, sales were what mattered. *We're running a retail business, not a museum,* she would always say.

"Attention, everyone!" Cynthia called out, making her way to the center of the room. "Thank you so much for joining us tonight. For those of you who haven't had a chance to meet our esteemed artist, may I present Mr. Thomas Malloy." She held her hand out for him to join her.

The room erupted in applause as he took a quick bow.

She continued, "For those not familiar with Thomas and his fabulous work, let me tell you a little bit about this amazing man. Mr. Malloy studied photography at New York City's prestigious School of the Visual Arts, and then went on to study with ..."

Carly sidled up to Ava and whispered, "Have you seen the price tags on these photos? Ten grand? Are you joking? Hell, I can take the same picture on my cell phone. You think Cynthia will let me hold an exhibit here?" She grabbed a handful of cold shrimp off of a passing tray and popped them in her mouth. "The snacks are pretty good, and so's the booze," she said as she washed the food down with the rest of her champagne, replacing her empty glass with a full one when the server walked by.

"How many of those have you had?"

"Who cares? They're free."

Ava shook her head. "No more ... please." Pulling the glass of bubbly liquid out of her hand, she put it back on the tray as the girl passed by them once again.

"So, thank you all so much for coming!" Cynthia continued. "Feel free to walk through the gallery at your leisure. If you have any questions, Thomas and I are happy to answer them, as is my assistant, Ava."

She stood up straighter at the mention of her name and waved slightly to acknowledge her position in the room. As she put her hand down, she caught his eye. *What the hell was he doing here ... with her?* Her heart fluttered. He looked remarkably handsome in a dark suit. Until tonight, she'd only seen him dressed in casual clothes or no clothes at all.

"Hey, Ava, isn't that Max?" Carly asked, following her stare. "Who's the babe he's with? Let's go say hi."

"Carly, no!" She snapped under gritted teeth, trying to pull her back. Unfortunately, it was too late. She'd already walked up to him and was pointing back to Ava. Before she knew it, her *friend* was practically dragging them over to where she was standing.

"Hey," she slurred, "I was right! It was Max. Still not sure about the chick, though."

"Max, Megan," Ava said, using her work voice, "Welcome."

"Oh, so you do know her. Oh wait, is this the tutor? The one he dumped you for? I didn't recognize her from the day we were spying on them in the library."

"Would you excuse us for a minute?" Ava pulled Carly into Cynthia's office. Shutting the door behind her, she picked up the phone, and called for a cab. "You will wait here until I come get you. Understand?"

Carly nodded, looking as if she were about to pass out.

"Good." She returned to the exhibit. Mortified, she rejoined Max and Megan, feeling as if she needed apologize. "Sorry about that," she murmured. "I'm afraid she was a bit too enthusiastic about the champagne."

They stood in awkward silence as people buzzed around them laughing and chatting, not noticing the tension that swirled around the trio.

"How was your exam?" Max finally asked.

"Oh, um, good, I think. The tricks you showed me really helped, I wish we had ..." She stopped herself. There was no point bringing up the past. Especially with Megan standing next to him, looking as if she were about to attack if Ava took one step closer.

He glanced down. "I'm sure Barry gave you a lot of help, too."

She'd forgotten about him, and the fact that Max had arranged to pay for her tutoring. "I told him I was okay on my own," she said.

He appeared disappointed, but she didn't care.

"So, um, what are you doing here?" Ava asked. "I mean ... never mind ... it's a public event, of course, I just didn't think you were in the market for high priced artwork."

"That's true. Sorry to say you won't be making any commission off of me tonight, but I'm actually a big fan. You know ... the whole flying planes and art thing? I have a few of his commercial prints."

"Right," she replied. "I didn't make the connection. Sorry."

"Yeah, and I didn't realize this was the same art gallery where you worked. Do you know Thomas Malloy?" he asked.

"Something like that." She noticed that Megan continued to move closer to Max as if she were marking her prey. Thus far, she had contributed nothing to the conversation, and Ava wondered what he saw in her – past the blonde Barbie doll facade. She didn't appear to like art or aviation. She supposed she answered her own question.

"Next time he walks by, I can introduce you if you'd like," she offered.

"Really?" he asked. "That would be amazing. Thanks."

"Sure thing," Ava told him, losing interest in the conversation. There didn't seem much point in pursuing even a friendship with him. He'd broken her heart and had obviously moved on. She needed to move on as well.

"Did anyone call a taxi?" a guy dressed in flannels, and looking sorely out of place, called out from the front door.

"Would you excuse me, please?"

She went into Cynthia's office to get Carly, who had fallen asleep at the desk. Putting Carly's arm around her neck, and her own arm around Carly's waist, Ava helped her out of the office and into the cab as discreetly as possible. Handing the man a twenty, which was more than enough for the short drive, she gave him instructions to get her home safely.

23

"Ava, dear, can I steal you away for a moment?" When she walked back into the gallery, Cynthia grabbed her arm.

"What's up?" Ava asked. Maybe Max and Megan would leave while she was gone, or at least get the hint and not wait around for her to return. She followed her boss into her office, hoping Carly hadn't messed anything up before she passed out.

"I've got buyers for five photos already. Can you get the paperwork ready for me?" She rattled off a list of the numbers for each one, knowing Ava would remember them all.

She smiled at her boss. The exhibit still had several hours to go. It was very possible she'd have to bring out some of the reserve photos before the night was over. That hardly ever happened. "Of course," she said, taking a seat behind the desk.

"Thanks. These buyers are like savages out there. They can't get enough. I don't want to leave them alone for a second. Just bring them out when you're done." Ava watched as Cynthia returned to the main gallery floor. Opening the drawer in the desk, she began pulling out the necessary papers.

"She's quite amazing, isn't she?"

"What?" Ava asked, startled to see Thomas standing in front of her with two flutes of champagne. "Oh, yes. She certainly knows what she's doing."

He handed her a glass.

"No thanks, I'm working," she said, feeling uncomfortable to be alone with him. Didn't he need to go back to the gallery to mingle with the crowd? She could always go introduce him to Max.

"Oh, come on now, you've worked so hard already, one drink will be okay. I'm sure Cynthia would approve. Five photos in the first hour ... I'd say that's something to celebrate."

Ava took the drink. She had a feeling Thomas wouldn't leave until she did. "Cheers!" he said, clinking his glass against hers. "We sure do make a great team."

She forced a smile and took a sip. "I don't know about that. You're the one with the talent. I've arranged plenty of exhibits that haven't sold nearly as well."

"I think you sell yourself short," he remarked. "Cynthia even pulled me aside a few minutes ago to tell me that the success of the opening is due, in part, to all of your hard work."

"You're too kind," she said, putting her glass down. She had a hard time believing anything he said anymore. She opened the desk drawer once more, searching for a pen.

"Do you like the champagne?" he asked, taking another sip, eyeing her over the rim of the flute. "It's from my private reserve, Perrier-Jouët. Nothing against your boss, but the champagne her caterer chose is horrid. You've barely touched yours. Go ahead, take another taste. You've never had anything like this, trust me."

She picked up the champagne and stared at the rising bubbles. *Oh, what the hell.* Maybe he'd leave and let her get her work done if she drank his fancy champagne. She took a long swig. It tasted like regular old champagne to her. Poor guy. He probably paid a small fortune for it. "It's great," she lied. "Thank you. I really do need to get these invoices done for Cynthia, now."

"I meant what I said the other day you know," he continued, walking over to shut the office door. "I can help you get a job here after you graduate. Cynthia and I are old friends. All I have to do is say the word, and it's yours."

Ava looked up at Thomas. His words sounded funny—as if he were in a tunnel—and the walls of the room were moving, too—in waves, going in first, then out. She blinked her eyes several times to clear her head.

"Thanks," she attempted to say. Her brain wanted to tell him that Cynthia offered her a job this afternoon, but she was unable to convince her voice to get the words out. What was happening?

He moved closer and came around to the side where she was sitting. "I don't know why you got so upset earlier, darling," he said, caressing her cheek. "Surely you knew I'd be leaving after the exhibit. We could've had a great week together, Ava, you and me. Why did you have to ruin everything?"

"Wha–I ..." Her head rolled to the side, despite her attempts to hold it straight.

He stepped directly next to her and turned her chair toward him. She willed her eyes to move toward the sound of a zipper opening. *Thomas' pants.* Suddenly, she felt his hands moving up her thighs as he pushed the fabric of her dress above her hips.

"No!" Ava tried to scream. The sound came out more as a muffled cry.

He straddled her, cupping her breasts and kissing her neck. "Don't fight it, darling. I know it's what you've wanted all along."

Her tears streamed down her face. "Please, no," she tried to say, but the words came out only as indistinguishable sounds. She tried to move her arms to push him away, but they hung down at her sides like two lead pipes. *What was wrong with her? Half a glass of champagne should not affect her like this.* She was unable to scream, unable to move.

Ava closed her eyes, feeling the weight of Thomas on top of her. Forcefully, he spread her legs apart, and pushed her panties to the side. There was nothing for her to do except cry and pray it would be over quickly. She waited to feel the pain of violation from this man she had liked, and even come to trust.

NO!

He couldn't do this to her. In one final attempt to save herself, she gathered all of her strength and cried, "NO! HELP!"

"What the *hell?*" The sound of a door banging against the wall like it had been thrown open hard filled the room.

In an instant, Thomas was gone, just gone. She heard the sound of his body being thrown against the wall as well as the punch that crushed bone before she opened her eyes.

"Are you okay?" Max rushed over to Ava's side and adjusted her dress.

Her head continued to roll to the side as she sobbed and attempted to nod.

"What's going on in here?" Cynthia demanded, running into her office. She rushed over to Thomas, who was nursing his already bruised and swollen jaw. She gasped when she noticed his pants down around his knees, and threw him a wrap that she kept hanging on her coat hook. "For God's sake, Thomas, cover yourself up."

"Call 9-1-1. Tell them we need an ambulance," Max ordered, cradling Ava, "and the police."

24

"How are you feeling?"

Ava looked around the room, her eyes desperately trying to focus on something, anything, as she wondered who was talking and why their voice was sending jagged waves of pain through her brain. She tried to lift her hand up to her head, hoping that would make the pounding stop, but felt restrained.

"Easy now, you don't want to pull out your IV," the kind voice said, smoothing her hair. "I imagine you have a bit of a headache. I can give you something for that if you'd like."

She nodded and felt relief within moments as the source of the voice injected a substance directly into the IV tubing.

"Thank you," she whispered, now able to focus on the nurse. "Where am I?"

"Parkside Hospital. The ambulance brought you in last night. Your boyfriend should be here soon, he just went to get some coffee. He's been by your side since you got here."

Flashes of the previous evening played in Ava's mind. The champagne, Thomas' advances, her inability to fight him off. "Thomas." In a panic, Ava tried to sit up. "He's not my boyfriend. I need to get out of here before he tries to …"

The nurse rubbed her shoulder as she tried to soothe her back into a lying position. "No, sweetie. His name isn't Thomas. It's Max. Everything is okay. You're safe here."

"Max is here?" she asked, her heart still pounding so hard it made her breathless. "Alone?"

She put her head back on the pillow and closed her eyes. Why was Max here? The last thing she remembered was Thomas on top of her, trying to push up her dress. She was yelling *no*. Well, her brain was yelling no. Did the words actually make it out of her mouth? She'd only had a small amount of the champagne he offered. Why had she felt so drunk last night? Not even drunk, really, she'd felt drugged. Had Thomas drugged her? She squeezed her eyes even tighter, not wanting to remember what happened next. There was a reason her brain pushed that memory to the back of her mind, and she wasn't ready to go there yet, although she was curious to know how Max wound up at the hospital with her.

"She's awake?" the male voice asked.

"Yes," replied the nurse. "You can go in. The doctor should be in soon as well."

Max pulled a chair close to Ava's bed and sat down.

"Hi there," he said, "Good to see you awake finally."

"Thanks."

"How are you?" Cautiously took hold of her hand, holding it tenderly.

"I feel like a truck hit me." She looked down and noticed his hand was swollen and bruised. "What happened to you? You look like you slugged the truck that hit me."

Max laughed. "Well, I kind of did. Don't you remember?"

"Not really."

Another memory flashed through her mind. It wasn't so much a vision as it was a sound ... the sound of two people scuffling. Were they throwing punches? Is that what Max meant?

"Hello there, Miss Haines, I'm Dr. Boyd." An older man in a white lab coat entered the room and walked up beside her bed.

"Call me Ava."

"Certainly, Ava." He nodded at Max. "Mr. Wallis, nice to see you again. Ava, I have some of your test results here. I'd like to go over them with you. Is Mr. Wallis a family member?"

"No," she replied, "but—" she looked back down to where her hand was cradled in his. "I guess he can stay. It's okay."

"All right, as long as you consent." The doctor flipped open her chart. "We ran a variety of tests on you after you were brought in. We were able to confirm Mr. Wallis' belief that no penetration took place."

She looked at Dr. Boyd and blinked several times.

"I wasn't raped?" She put her head back against the pillow as a huge wave of relief overtook her body.

"No," he confirmed. "Do you remember the attack?"

"Not all of it. Not that part of it. I mean, I wasn't sure."

Max smiled at her and wiped away the single tear that slid down her cheek.

"The other good news is that there were no signs of any drugs in your blood stream. However, your blood alcohol level was .25. That's extremely high. Dangerously high, actually. Especially for someone of your size."

"But I only had two sips of champagne. That's it. I didn't even want to have it. Thomas kept insisting. He said we needed to celebrate and that this champagne was some fancy stuff from his own private stash. I swear I didn't have anything else to drink. I never drink when I'm working."

Dr. Boyd took off his glasses and sat down in a chair next to Max. "Ava, did Thomas also drink the champagne?"

"Yes," she replied. "He had more than I did. He had the entire glass. I only had about half."

"Did you see him pour both drinks from the same bottle?" he asked.

"No. He came into my boss' office holding two glasses that already had champagne in them. He offered one to me, and he drank from the other."

"And what happened after you took the first sip?" Dr. Boyd asked.

Ava thought for a moment. The events of last night were still so muddled in her brain—it took a few moments to bring them into focus.

"Nothing right away. The first sip I took was so tiny. Like I said, I didn't want any to begin with. I was trying to get some paperwork done, but he kept insisting. I only took a sip hoping it would make him happy so he would leave. But then he kept going on and on about how fancy and expensive the champagne was. He was making me feel bad that I wasn't drinking it ... like he was being so generous to offer it to me, and I was just wasting it. So I took another sip, a bigger sip."

"Then what happened?"

"Then I started feeling funny."

"How so?"

"I don't know ... sort of drunk, but not really. I felt *different*. The walls were moving like waves, and my head got really heavy. I remember I felt like my neck was an elastic band or something. No matter how hard I tried, I couldn't hold my head up. I couldn't really speak either. My brain would form words, but my mouth wouldn't get the words out. After that my memory is a little fuzzy to tell you the truth."

Dr. Boyd patted my hand. "How are you feeling now?"

"Better, especially since the nurse gave me something for my headache. Will I be going home today?"

"I don't see why not. You have an appointment with a counselor before you leave this morning. After that, I know the police will want a statement, and then we'll sign your release papers."

"Police?" Ava asked, eyes wide.

"Just tell them the truth, there's nothing to worry about."

"Dr. Boyd," Max started, "if Ava only had two sips of champagne, why was her blood alcohol level so high?"

"There are lots of reasons why one person may metabolize alcohol slower or faster than another—factors such as size, whether or not they had anything to eat, medical conditions, and the like. However, to see such an extreme level after only two sips, honestly it doesn't make sense to me. Is it possible this Thomas fellow put something in her drink that acted as a catalyst to boost the effects of the alcohol ... something he knew wouldn't show up in her blood if she were to be tested? I suppose. The problem is, I can't prove it one way or another without the numbers to back me up."

"There's something else," Ava said. At the time it seemed odd, but now it was starting to make sense.

"What is it?" asked Dr. Boyd.

"We went out for dinner last weekend. I had three drinks. Normally, I'd be fine, but I got drunk. *Really drunk.*"

"Did you leave the table at any time that night?" Max asked.

She thought for a moment. "Yes, actually, right after the third drink arrived, I got a call from my younger sister, Tessa. I excused myself to talk to her. I was only gone for a few minutes. I felt fine at that point. It wasn't until I came back to have that third drink that I started feeling weird. Do you think ... It just doesn't make sense. He was such a gentlemen that night."

"Again, without labs, I really can't say," Dr. Boyd remarked. "But be sure and tell all of that to the police."

Ava nodded.

The doctor made a few more notes and then said, "You take care of yourself. Be sure to follow up with your regular doctor in the next week or so, okay? Mr. Wallis, thank you for bringing her in."

25

"You don't have to do this, you know."

Max arranged the flowers Cynthia had sent over in the vase while Ava rested on her couch. They looked a million times nicer than the ones Thomas had sent yesterday before her exam. Those were now outside rotting in the dumpster.

Once Dr. Boyd signed all of the papers releasing her from the hospital, Max had given her a ride back to her apartment. He'd grabbed the pillow and blanket from her bed, made sure she was comfortable, and then served her the sandwich he'd picked up at the deli on the way home. After that, he busied himself around her tiny apartment, which included taking on the task of arranging the enormous bouquet of flowers that were waiting on her doorstep.

She was relieved she'd left her apartment in a somewhat decent state. Well, decent might have been an exaggeration, but at least there were no dirty panties or bras strewn across the floor. Her mother would be almost proud.

She desperately wanted to call Holly, but at the same time was hesitant. For starters, she didn't want her sister to overreact—something that surely would happen. Should she call Tessa instead? No, her youngest sister was only in high school. It wasn't fair to dump something like this on her. It had to be Holly ... privately. With Max wandering about, even the bathroom afforded little privacy in her minuscule apartment. Even so, she didn't want to ask him to leave, not after everything he'd done for her. Not yet. The truth was, she was afraid to be alone.

Max continued to fuss over the flowers, even though they were fine. "How does this look?"

Ava smiled. Either he sensed she didn't want to be alone, or he wanted to be here with her. Any of those reasons were okay with her, just as long as he stayed, although she kind of hoped for option two.

"They look great. Thank you—for everything." She felt tears coming to her eyes. She wanted to say so much more, but it was so hard for her to talk about last night. When she'd met with the counselor earlier, all of the remaining memories flooded her brain, including the one where Max came in and pulled Thomas off of her, saving her.

He sat on the edge of the couch, close, but not too close. "I know, and it's okay. You don't have to say anything. I've been a real jerk to you. You don't owe me a thank you. If anything, I owe you an apology."

The tears flowed freely down her face. Why was she crying? Was it because of last night? Was it because Max admitted he'd been a jerk and wanted to apologize? Was it because she was happy he was sitting here with her now, looking at her the way he was? Just how was he looking at her? Was she mistaking pity for tenderness?

Ava turned away, recalling the hostility she felt when she received the letter from Max the day after their date. "You should probably check in with Megan. I'm sure she's wondering where you've been all this time."

He sighed. "We're not a couple. She was just my tutor."

"Same way you were just mine?"

"I guess I asked for that."

"You brought her to the exhibit. It looked like a date to me."

"Maybe it did, but I promise you, we weren't dating. That was the first time I'd been anywhere with her but the library. I'd mentioned I was going, and she asked if she could come along. I don't know why, though. She seemed completely bored by the entire thing once we got there."

Ava laughed and turned back toward him. "She really did look miserable. Although, I suppose she liked you enough to give it a try."

Max shrugged. "The feeling wasn't mutual. She was a good tutor, but that's it." He sounded sincere. Was that all there was between them? Were they truly just teacher and student? Maybe, but that still didn't explain why he deserted her days before her own exam.

"You were a good tutor, too," Ava said, looking away.

"I'm sorry. I just … I couldn't … I—"

Ava's phone buzzed before Max could finish. He picked it up and handed it to her.

"It's a text from Cynthia," she said after reading the brief message.

"I forgot to tell you that she called while you were with the counselor this morning. I hope you don't mind, but I answered your phone and spoke with her."

She desperately wanted to continue the conversation with Max about why he wrote the letter, but she'd been waiting to talk to Cynthia as well. She knew she would have news about Thomas. She'd have to come back to the conversation with Max as soon as she had a chance.

"What did she say? Ava asked.

"The police came to see her also. Apparently, after they arrested Thomas, he gave Cynthia's name as a character witness. She refused to speak on his behalf, and stuck up for you instead. Anyway, she wanted to let you know that she pulled Thomas' exhibit. You don't need to stay in town all week now."

Ava nodded. "So they have him in custody," she stated. She should have felt elated, but all it did was drive home the fact that someone she'd put her trust in had tried to attack her. Still, she did feel somewhat safer knowing the police had him.

"Yes. Cynthia says the story has made national news since he's so high profile ... although your name has been left out. The police tested the champagne and confirmed it was laced. Several other women have already come forward. It seems he's made a habit out of giving unsuspecting women his *special* champagne. They all have similar stories though they weren't as fortunate as you. The prosecutor is already working on his case. Cynthia says he'll be in jail for a long time."

Ava sighed in relief. "That's good news."

"I'm sorry I didn't tell you sooner. I wasn't sure you were up for a chat about him, yet. So what does Cynthia have to say?"

She looked down at the message from her boss:

"Never trust a man who is more impressed with himself than anyone else ... Now Max, there's a man you can trust. Hope you are feeling better xoxo"

"She just hopes I feel better," Ava replied.

26

"Ava! Ava! Open up!"

The pounding on the door was an unwelcome reminder that her headache was not quite gone. She looked at Max and threw her head back down on the pillow.

"It's all right. You can let her in. She's not going to go away until you do." Propping herself up, she prepared for the drama.

Carly shoved the door open the moment Max released the latch—not even waiting for him to open it for her. She rushed to the couch "Oh my God! Are you okay? What happened?" she demanded, kneeling and taking one of Ava's hands in hers.

"I'm fine, I promise." Carly looked like she was on the verge of hysterics and it was just more than she could handle right now. "Shouldn't you be on a bus heading home?" she asked, hoping the calm tone in her voice might reassure her friend.

"I couldn't go without making sure you were okay. It's all over the news. I changed my ticket. I didn't want to leave you all alone until I knew you were good." She looked up, noticing Max for the first time since she'd walked in to the apartment. "But I see you're not. Alone that is. What's going on?"

"Why don't you tell me what's going on. What exactly did you hear on the news? Cynthia said my name wasn't mentioned."

"It wasn't," Carly told her, still staring at Max, her expression confused. She shook her head slightly and brought her eyes back down to Ava. "All the news said was that the photographer of the *Images in Flight* exhibit, Thomas Malloy, sexually assaulted Cynthia Simms' assistant at the gallery's opening last night. That's you, right?"

"Yes. Except it was only an attempted sexual assault thanks to Max. Other than Thomas drugging me, I'm relatively fine. Max rescued me before any real damage was done … well, to me at least. Thomas wasn't so lucky." She pointed to his bruised and swollen hand.

"I hope you hit him where it counts."

"I didn't really have time to think about it," Max explained. "I was mostly concerned about getting him off Ava. But I did hear a pretty good crack when my fist made contact with his jaw." He smiled, proud of himself.

"Not exactly the body part I was thinking of, but that works, too," Carly said. "So you sure you're okay?" she turned her attention back to her friend.

"Yeah. I'm a bit shaken up, but the doc at the hospital gave me some good drugs to help me relax. My happy pills." She picked up the prescription bottle and pretended to gulp the entire contents, before Max scooped the container out of her hand.

"I think I'll be in charge of these for the time being," he said, putting them in his pocket.

"So, Max, you're going to stay here for a while?" Carly asked, looking at Ava as she waited for the answer.

"If Ava wants me to," he replied. "I'd planned on staying in Wolfenson this week anyway."

"Is that what you want?" Carly asked her. "Because I can change my schedule, it's no big deal. Or I can call Holly for you. You have options. Whatever *you're* comfortable with."

Ava looked from Carly to Max and back to Carly again. "It's fine if he stays. I know you're anxious to get home, and I'll probably head home soon myself. Cynthia closed down the exhibit so I don't need to be here this week after all. I can join my family at any time. I just need to rest for a bit before I start packing."

"Okay. If you're sure. So … does this mean you two are—"

"Carly!" Ava exclaimed, shaking her head sharply. "Don't you have a bus to catch?"

"All right. All right. I'm just trying to keep up with you, Av, that's all. I've lost track."

"I'm warning you," she said, glancing pointedly toward the door.

"Got it. I'm done. Anyway, yeah, there's a bus in an hour, so I need to run, but text me if you need anything … even if you just want to chat, okay? Or, you know, update me." She motioned her head toward Max, and Ava rolled her eyes. "I mean it, Av. You take care of yourself. Love you. I'll see you in a month." Carly gave her friend a big hug before walking up to Max. "Don't do anything stupid," she whispered to him before walking out the door.

"She's a charming one," he noted, as he closed the door behind her.

Ava put her head back down on her pillow. "Do you think I can take one of those pills now?"

27

"No! No!" Ava thrashed about restlessly, gasping for air as she woke up to find herself in Max's arms.

"It's okay, it was just a dream. You're safe." He stroked her hair as she tried to calm her breathing. "I'm not going to let anything happen to you." He kissed the top of her head softly, and she relaxed her body into his, grateful to feel his arms wrapped around her.

"It wasn't *all* a dream, was it?" she asked tearfully. "He really did attack me. He really did almost—"

"Shh ..." he murmured, slowly rocking her. "He can't hurt you anymore. Not now, and not ever.

Ava pulled away slowly, looking up at him. "Max," a single tear slid down her cheek and landed perfectly still on her top lip, "I never really had a chance to thank you. I mean, you've done so much. I don't know what—"

Gently, he put his fingers up to her mouth to wipe away the tear. "You don't have to say anything." He gazed at her, and she understood that everything she wanted to say, everything she couldn't say, he could read in her eyes. The apology he started earlier wasn't important anymore. The only thing that mattered at the moment was that he was here – with her.

As if breaking a spell, she sat up and glanced around. The sun had long since gone down. "What time is it?" she asked.

"Around ten o'clock, why?"

"I've been asleep that long? Carly left around two. I guess I'm not going home today."

"No, I imagine your parents wouldn't want you showing up after midnight."

"It's probably better anyway. I'm not feeling a hundred percent yet, and I'm certainly not ready to answer all of their questions right now. I'm sure Holly's seen the news and has figured out I'm the one who was attacked. Hell, if Carly could figure it out, anyone can."

Max laughed.

"Speaking of my sister," Ava said, looking around, "do you know where my phone is?"

"I moved it to the kitchen counter. It was buzzing and beeping non-stop. I didn't want it to wake you." He grabbed it and handed it back to her.

Max was right. Ava had what seemed like an unending stream of messages and calls. The calls were all from Holly, which meant she either knew or suspected. The text messages were a hodgepodge from Tessa, Holly, and Carly.

Carly: OMG, girlfriend, what is going on between you and the hunk? He better be taking good care of you. Text me back.

Holly: How was your exam? Mine sucked, but it's over. Hope the opening was a huge hit. Wish you were coming home this week xoxo.

Tessa: When r u coming home? Mom & Dad r driving me totes nuts. Have big news about cute boy in chem class. Mwah.

Holly: Are you okay? Just saw on news about an attack at a gallery. It wasn't you, was it? Text me back—love you. xoxo

Carly: This bus ride is taking forever! Cute guy 4 rows up, I'm going for it. Wish me luck. Still waiting to hear about you and Max.

Tessa: Boys suck. My friend Juls saw cute boy from chem class at mall with slut from 11th grade. When *are* u coming home? Miss u!!

Holly: You're scaring me. Why aren't you answering your phone or your texts? Are you okay? I wish I could remember the name of the gallery you worked at! Damn. Please text or call! Love you.

Carly: So Mr. 4th row hottie claims to have a wife. Whatever. I'm going to try to take a nap for the rest of the ride. Hope you're having fun *wink wink.

"Everything okay?" Max asked.

"Mostly," Ava answered. "My sister is worried about me. I really need to call her. Do you mind?"

"Oh," he said, looking around the small apartment. "I can go wait outside if you want."

"No, it's okay. You can stay."

"Well, how about I fix you something to eat then?" he offered. "You must be hungry. I'm not the best cook, but I know how to make spaghetti. I think I saw a box in your cabinet earlier when I was looking for a glass for water."

"That would be great. Thanks."

She watched for a minute as he fumbled around the kitchen and giggled to herself before picking up the phone. She supposed she had to get this call over with eventually. Slowly, she dialed Holly's number and prepared herself. The phone only rang half a ring.

"Ava? What took you so long? I've been worried sick! Are you okay? Was that your gallery in the news? Were you the person attacked? Isn't that the Thomas guy you told me about? What happened? Why didn't you call me back? Ava! *Why aren't you answering me?*"

She took a deep breath and let it out slowly before answering. "Can I speak now?" she asked and continued before giving her sister a chance to respond. "I'm okay. Yes, that was my gallery, and yes, I was the one who was attacked—"

"Oh my God!" her sister shrieked.

Ava pulled the phone away from her ear. She knew there would be drama— she just wasn't expecting it to be so loud. "Holly! Let me finish." She took another long breath. "It wasn't exactly like they were reporting on the news. He didn't rape me or anything."

"Oh, thank goodness," she said, sighing in relief. "So what did happen?"

Ava retold the story again. Between the doctor at the hospital, the counselor, the police, Carly, and now Holly, she had told the story five times already today. It didn't get any easier as the day went on.

"That's unbelievable. He seemed like such a decent guy. Especially after he took you home the night you got drunk."

"I know," she agreed. "The police think he might have drugged me that night, too."

"No! Are you kidding me? But you told me he was a perfect gentleman that night."

"He was. The officer I spoke with said he may have been testing my system. You know, to see how I reacted to the drug ... sort of a trial run. Max thinks he was either trying to gain my trust or trying to build up his own character, as if he knew he might get caught at some point."

"Wow, that's crazy. Wait a minute. Max?"

"Well, yes. He spoke to the police also. He was a witness to part of it, remember?" She wasn't quite ready to mention that he hadn't left her side since the incident took place. That would just bring up an entirely new line of questions she didn't want to answer, especially with Max in earshot.

"Right. So, the news report says others have come forward, and Thomas has been arrested," Holly said.

"Yes. He's already in jail."

"Good! Are you sure you're all right? Do you want me to come stay with you? I was going home tomorrow, but I can head out your way instead."

Ava glanced into the kitchen. Max furiously moved back and forth between two pots on the stove. The water from the boiling pasta of the first pot bubbled over the sides, while a second pot on the stove spewed tomato sauce all over his shirt and chin. He looked up at her and waved.

"No, it's not necessary, but thanks for offering," she said, smiling. "I've got a friend staying with me. As soon as I'm up for it, I'll make the drive home. Do me a favor and don't tell Mom and Dad. I'm pretty sure they don't know, or they would have called by now. No need to worry them. I'm really fine, honest."

"All right, sis. But if you change your mind, I'm only a phone call away. See you soon. Love you."

"Love you, too."

28

"So, you haven't said much," Max said as they sat at her tiny table eating the supper he'd prepared. "Is it that bad?"

"What?" Ava asked, twirling the last of the pasta around on her fork. "Oh, no, the spaghetti is just fine, thanks. It's been a crazy twenty-four hours, huh?"

"That's for sure."

"It's getting kind of late," she said, looking out the window. "I ... um ... well..."

"What is it? Is something wrong? Do you want me to go?"

She put her fork down and looked at him. "No. Unless ... do you need to go? We never discussed how long you planned to stay or anything. I just ... I guess this is kind of awkward, you know, for sleeping arrangements."

She glanced around her one room apartment. Her bed, a futon on a platform that never folded up as intended, was pushed against the back wall. Squeezed in to the rest of the compact floor space were her sofa, coffee table, TV stand, dresser, and the little dining table that also doubled as her desk. A small galley kitchen lined the left wall, while a tiny closet, and the door to the even tinier bathroom lined the right wall. The accommodations weren't exactly lush, nor were they designed for overnight guests who wouldn't be sharing the bed.

"I can take the couch. It's no big deal," he said.

"No, no. I'm already set up there, and it's not even full size—it's more like a loveseat. You'll be all scrunched up. You take the bed, I insist."

"Absolutely not," Max stated. "I've slept in chairs and been just fine. This is perfect. And I can stay for as long as you need ... until you go back home, or until someone else comes to stay with you. Isn't that what we agreed to when Carly was here? Really, I don't mind."

Ava nodded, grateful he was staying true to his word, and glad they had worked out sleeping arrangements. The thought of spending the night alone was beyond terrifying.

"Good. I will need to go back to my place in the morning to get my toothbrush and some clean clothes, though." He smiled. "Otherwise, you might just kick me out. I can get a little stinky. But you can come with me if you don't want to be alone."

"I'm sure I'll be fine for a half hour or so. Anyway, if you start to get stinky, I'll just spray you with room freshener," she laughed. "I really do appreciate all that you're doing for me. Are you sure you don't want the bed?"

"Positive," he said, finishing the spaghetti on his plate in a final bite.

The next morning, Ava woke to the smell of eggs and coffee.

"You do know how to cook something other than spaghetti," she said as she walked over to the kitchen.

Max smiled. "Spaghetti and eggs. That's pretty much it. You've now seen my entire repertoire. Oh, and I can brew a mean cup of coffee, too. Want some?"

"Thanks." She grabbed two mugs out of the cabinet and began pouring. "How do you like yours? I don't know if I have milk that's any good, but I've got that nasty powder stuff. I swiped a bunch of packets from the student center last week."

"Perfect," he responded. "Coffee with nasty powder stuff. That's exactly how I take my coffee, anyway. I kid you not."

Ava laughed, putting her hand up to her mouth to hide her morning breath. "Me too, actually. We'll both be nuclear in about twenty years from the chemicals they put in that crap."

"Ten is more likely. Here you go. I wasn't sure how you liked your eggs. Scrambled okay?"

"Scrambled is great," she answered, feeling so comfortable having him there she didn't care that she was in her pajamas, or that her hair was probably a crazy mess. Even the morning breath could wait until after they'd eaten.

They sat down at the table together and started eating.

"Looks like you slept well," he said, crunching into a slice of slightly burnt toast. "I was keeping one ear open in case you had any more bad dreams."

Ava sighed. "I knew you weren't going to sleep well on that couch wanna-be. Tonight you take the bed."

"No way. I'm a light sleeper. It had nothing to do with the couch."

"If you're sure..." She hesitated for a moment then asked, "You don't have to be heading home for the holidays?"

"I'm not in any rush. My family is better taken in small doses. A month at home is a long time."

She giggled. "Ah, one of those types of families? An Uncle Eddie that everyone avoids and flying Christmas china in the middle of dinner?"

Max smiled broadly. "So you've met them! Yeah, that's pretty much how it goes. You left out the part about my mom getting on my case from the moment I walk through the door about how I really should be thinking about going into law or medicine instead of setting my sights on pilot school. And then there's Aunt Sheila who always asks, 'Why don't you have a serious girlfriend yet, Maxie, hmm? Are you gay? Because if you are, I have a lovely boy I can introduce you to'."

"No!" Ava laughed so hard, her eyes began to water.

"Yup. So you can see why I'm not in a big hurry to rush home."

"I guess not," she said, wiping her eyes.

"Anyway, as soon as I help you clean up, I have to run out for a little bit. Are you sure you'll be okay alone? You could come with me."

"No, I'll be fine. I have to get used to being by myself eventually." She paused and added, "You won't be long, right?"

"Maybe an hour," he said. "I need to swing by my apartment to grab a few things, then go up to campus to see if grades are posted. On the way back, I'll stop by the market to pick up a few groceries. I promise to keep my phone with me at all times."

"I'll be okay, really." She stood up to help him clear the dishes, and as she followed him into the kitchen said, "So, um, you're not, are you?"

"Not what?" he asked, washing the plates.

She grinned at him. "Gay."

"No!" He threw the sponge at her and laughed.

29

Ava paced the floor. Max had only been gone ten minutes. Why did it feel like ten hours? *Ugh.* She should have gone with him. It was too soon for her to be alone. *Thomas is in custody. You're fine, Ava.* She checked the door again. Locked. She had given Max a key in case she decided to take a nap. Oh, who was she kidding? She'd never be able to fall asleep. Holly. Holly could help keep her mind busy. She just needed someone to distract her.

She picked up her phone and dialed her sister's number. *Pick up, Hol. Pick up!*

"Hi, you've reached Holly Haines. Sorry I missed your call. Please leave a message. *Beep.*"

"Hey, Hol, it's Ava. Everything's fine. Just checking in. Call me. Love you."

Carly or Tessa? Did she want twenty-year-old drama or sixteen-year-old drama? Carly would ask too many questions about Max. Tessa it was, although she doubted she'd be up this early on a Sunday morning. She dialed again. Her little sister would forgive her for waking her up.

"Ava? Is that you? Are you on your way home? Please say you are. Mom and Dad are driving me nuts!"

"Hey—yeah, it's me. No, sorry, I'm stuck here another few days. So what's going on? Are you still upset about that boy from chemistry class?"

"Who? Oh, him? No. He can go suck it."

"Nice language, Tessa."

"What? I can say a lot worse you know."

"Yes, I know," she said. Sometimes she felt like she and her sister lived worlds apart. She supposed having six years between them had that effect.

"Anyway, he's not worth crying over," Tessa added.

"Good. I'm glad to hear it. Are you studying for midterms?"

"Trying to. That's the part where Mom and Dad are driving me crazy. It would be a lot easier if they didn't keep trying to *help*."

Ava laughed. "Yeah, I remember their version of help. Dad always wanted to explain stuff completely differently than the teacher taught it. Mom had this incessant need to test me on the material every ten minutes, and then she'd get angry because I didn't know it. When I would try to explain that I would know it if she'd give me enough time to study, she'd get all insulted. You'd think with kid number three, they'd have gotten the hint."

"Well they haven't. I was hoping you'd be here to give me a little back up."

"What about Holly? Isn't she coming home today?" she asked.

"Yeah, but you know, ever since she decided to become a teacher, she wants to get in and *help*, too. So now I've got three of them. Anyway, I gotta run. I'm at work. My boss already warned me once today about my phone."

Ava looked at the clock. It was nine-fifteen. She'd forgotten that Tessa worked the breakfast shift at the local diner on Sundays. Ava didn't envy her one bit. She'd had the same job when she was sixteen. The customers were either coming in drunk from a night of partying, hungover, or both.

"Okay, sweets. I'll see you in a few days. Hang in there! Love you."

"Love you back, bye."

Ten more minutes gone … forty or so to go.

Ava sat on the couch and flipped on the television. Maybe some cheesy morning talk show would relax her, or she could take one of those pills—if she could find them. While she sat and contemplated her options, a noise coming from outside the front of her apartment diverted her attention. She watched as the doorknob to her front door jiggled. Her phone sat only inches away, but she couldn't reach for it. Her entire body felt paralyzed but for the pounding of her heart.

Louder, louder, louder—she couldn't concentrate on anything except the pounding and the knob. She watched as it slowly started to turn. The door creaked as it began to open ... steadily, deliberately. She heard the scream, but wasn't conscious of the fact that it came from her body. She no longer had control of her movements or reactions.

"Ava! It's just me!" the familiar voice rang out. Running to the couch, he grabbed her shoulders, trying to get her to focus on his face. "It's Max. Can you hear me?"

She stopped screaming and stared blankly at his kind face, as what he was saying registered with her. She burst into tears and wrapped her arms around his neck. "I thought you were—" She stopped and gasped for air, as if trying to fill her lungs for the very first time.

"I'm *so* sorry. I went to campus first, and when I was on my way to my apartment, I felt bad about leaving you alone. I decided to come back to get you. I should have called. I'm sorry. I didn't mean to scare you." He hugged her close, not letting go until the last of her trembles subsided.

30

"Are you feeling better?" Max put the cup of tea on the table and sat next to Ava on the couch.

"Yes," she smiled, "I'm sorry. I feel ridiculous. I totally overreacted."

He took her hands in his own. "You had a very traumatic experience just over twenty-four hours ago. I think you're entitled to be a little jumpy."

"That was more than a little jumpy. That was like horror movie theatrics."

"You have some good lungs on you, that's for sure," he told her, reaching up to smooth her hair.

Ava wished he would hold her again. Just for a little while. Searching for something to take her mind off it, she said, "So you stopped by campus to see if your grades were posted. Were they?"

A huge smiled appeared on his face. "Some of them."

"I'm gathering by your expression that you did quite well," she said, smiling, too. She couldn't help it. His good mood was contagious. It was just what she needed to help her feel better.

"I did okay," he replied, still beaming.

Ava cocked her head and wondered what he was up to. "Why the goofy grin then?"

"Promise not to get upset?"

"I don't know yet," she cautiously responded.

"Well, as I was walking down the hall of the business department getting ready to leave, Professor Eisen was coming out of his office holding a sheet of paper."

"And," she asked, getting worried.

"And it was his final exam grades. He was posting them on his door. Anyway, I honestly was only going to look for mine, but then my eyes just sort of slipped three columns over into the Statistics 101 class, and I may have wandered down until I found your name."

"Uh-huh," she said, smirking. "Well, let's get the news over with. Am I looking at summer school?"

He paused for a minute, the corners of his lips still in a smirk.

"Max!" she shouted, smacking him in the shoulder. "Tell me already!"

"You got an eighty-seven!"

"*What?*" she shrieked. "Are you sure? Haines. H-A-I-N-E-S. You were looking at the score for Haines?"

"Yes, I was looking at Haines! *Ava Haines.* You. Got. An. Eighty. Seven!"

Ava flew into his lap, pushing him down until he was lying on the cushions, holding him at bay with her hands on his shoulders. She stared down at him with wide eyes as he looked back in shock. "Oh my God! I can't believe this! I never! I mean, I thought I might have gotten in the sixties, but an eighty-seven? You know this is because of what you taught me, don't you?"

Without realizing what she was doing, she brought her head down into the crook of his neck and began to kiss him just below his ear. Softly at first, but then more passionately. Trailing her lips across his cheek, she eventually reached his already parted lips. *Those lips.* The lips she'd waited so long to taste once more.

She knew then she wouldn't let him get away again. She *couldn't* let him get away again. Max wrapped his arms around her, pulling her in even closer with long drawn out kisses, exploring her delicate lips with his tongue. Their breathing synced into one melody as their bodies pressed together almost as one.

"No," Max groaned, abruptly thrusting her back while trying to catch his breath. He could barely look her in the eyes. "We can't."

Ava sat up, looking away. "I don't understand," she said softly, curling up against the arm of the sofa, the feeling of rejection taking over once more.

He tried to take her hand, but she pulled it to the side and placed it in her lap, guarding it from any further intrusion. This wasn't happening again.

"Ava," he began, then muttered something under his breath before saying, "I need to explain to you why I sent Barry in to the library with that note the day after our date. I should have been honest with you right away. I don't know why it's taken me so long to tell you this. Well, I do know. At first I didn't want to distract you from your studies. Then the attack with Thomas happened, and I started to tell you, but Carly showed up, and—"

She shook her head in disbelief. The connection, the passion—she wasn't imagining those things. Wasn't he feeling them too? "Just tell me … please. Just tell me so I can pack and go home. Then you won't have to waste your time playing bodyguard and pretending you care about me."

"It's not like that, Ava."

She felt the sting of tears and tried to blink them away. *Don't let him see you cry, damn it.* "So what's it like, then?"

He paused, as if trying to find the right words. "Remember how I told you I wanted to go to flight school to become a pilot after graduation?"

"Yes," she said through her muffled sobs.

"Well, I heard about a school out in California that was accepting seniors who were close to graduating. They have a program that lets you overlap your final semester of college with your beginning courses of flight school. It seemed like a really great deal, and it's one of the top flight schools in the country. It's very competitive. I knew I had little chance of getting in, but I applied anyway. This was months ago—before we ever met."

Ava wiped her eyes, then turned and glanced at Max, wondering what any of this had to do with his inability to kiss her more than once without running away.

"Anyway, the day of our first date, I got a letter from them. It was a thin envelope. You know what they say about thin envelopes."

She nodded. "Rejection letters."

"Exactly," he agreed. "I didn't want it to spoil my evening with you, so I threw it on my bed and forgot about it. It definitely didn't spoil my evening. We had a great night. In fact, that was probably the best first date I've ever been on."

"You have a hell of a way of showing it."

"I know, I'm sorry," he replied. "See, the thing is, when I got back to my place, I opened the letter. I was on such a high from our date, I knew that even a rejection wouldn't spoil my good mood. Only it wasn't a rejection. I was accepted into the program. The packet of materials—all of those papers and things that normally make the envelope so thick—are now online. Got to love technology, I guess."

"So that's great, Max," Ava said, unable to keep the bitterness from her tone. "You got everything you wanted, and I got stiffed. No tutor and no boyfriend. Forgive me, but I'm still not making the connection between you getting in, and you not speaking to me ever again."

"Don't you see? The school is in California, and the program starts in January. I have to move all the way across the country in a few weeks. It wouldn't be fair to you, then or now, to start a relationship. I'd just be leading you on."

"Well, what about now? What the hell do you call what you're doing now?" she asked, not sure if she was angry with Max, the situation, or both. Once again, she found herself in a position of falling for someone who would be leaving. Only this was different. This was so different. With Max there were *sparks*, he was someone worth fighting for ... someone worth waiting for.

He twisted his hands together in his lap. "I don't know. I guess it's like you said. I feel like I'm your bodyguard. Like it's my job to protect you. But I'm not pretending to care for you. I really do—" The anguish in his voice gave her the answer she was looking for. He did feel the same way about her.

She reached up to curl his hair between her fingers. "Can't you see? We're meant to be with each other. The more we try to stay apart, the more we're pushed together. I know you feel it, too."

He looked at her and nodded, and she could swear she saw tears in his eyes.

"Except there's nothing that's going to push the east coast and west coast closer together," he said softly, looking as though he wished there were a way to make that magically happen.

"Lots of couples have long distance relationships. It's doable if you believe in it … if you believe in us," she insisted. It certainly wasn't ideal, but it wasn't the end of the world either. It wouldn't be forever. "How long is the program?"

"With finishing up my degree, just over a year."

"That's not long at all. The question is—if you weren't going away, would you be willing to give us a chance?"

"In a heartbeat," he answered. "Having to push you away like this is killing me."

"Then don't, Max. Don't push me away." She took his hands in hers and tugged him toward her, aching to taste his lips, aching to taste every inch of him. Yet she only stared into his eyes … eyes that revealed to her just how much he cared, that still had so much to share. He nodded slowly, allowing Ava to pull him up.

Without hesitation or doubt, she led him to her bed, giving her whole self to the man she had desired from the moment their eyes met in the courtyard, whether she'd been willing to admit it at the time or not.

31

A va loved being in Wolfenson while the majority of the student population was gone. She felt like she and Max had the entire town to themselves. They didn't have to wait for a table at The Spot, they didn't have to fight for parking, and they could get prime seats to see a movie at the normally packed multiplex theater.

They spent every moment together, shopping, walking through town after dark to ooh and ah over the festive decorations, or just hanging out in one or the other's apartments. Noticeably absent from their itinerary was a visit to the gallery.

Max suggested going there almost daily, telling her it would be good to both see Cynthia, and renew her faith in the one place she most enjoyed spending her time. She knew he was right. The gallery was her happy place. She needed to disassociate it somehow from the attack. Ava tried several times to will herself to go, but each time, she managed to make an excuse. *It's too late, by the time we get there it'll be closed,* or *not today, I still need to finish my holiday shopping.* As a last resort, she'd nibble on Max's ears and playfully bite his lips— leading him to the bedroom where he'd forget all about his plan to help her heal from the attack.

It wasn't that she didn't want to see her boss—she just wasn't ready to face the rush of memories that would surely return the moment she set foot inside the gallery, the scene of the crime. She didn't want to spend her week thinking about old and traumatic memories with Thomas, when she could be spending it making new and wonderful memories with Max.

"What about this?" she asked, holding up a bright pink sweater.

"It's not really my color," Max answered grinning as he took it from her and held it against his chest.

"Not for you! For Tessa," she said, grabbing it back. She held it up, looking at it with a critical eye. "She's so hard to shop for. Actually, this would be better for Holly. Tessa's not really a pink kind of girl.

Maybe makeup. Last time I was home she rifled through my stash and swiped all my good stuff."

Max grabbed her around the waist and held her tight. "You should've given it all to her, you don't need it. You're a natural beauty."

He pulled her between two racks of clothes, where they'd be out of sight from the other shoppers and kissed her—the kind of kiss that made her want to find an empty dressing room for them to sneak into. Except then she'd have to stop kissing him, and that just wasn't an option. She couldn't stop. Her body wouldn't let her.

The security guard, however, had no problem putting a swift end to their too public make out session. He grabbed each of their shoulders and forcefully pulled them apart. "You're going to have to take that outside," he said gruffly.

Ava could barely breathe, she was so worked up, but Max looked completely calm—and a little proud. He smiled at the burly man. "Certainly, sir. We're sorry." He took Ava's hand and began to lead her toward the exit door.

The security guard once again grabbed their shoulders just as they reached the doors. He nodded toward the pink sweater, still in Ava's hand.

"Ma'am," he said. "I hope you were planning on paying for that."

"Oh!" she exclaimed. Her cheeks, which already flushed from the first encounter with the security guard, felt as if they were now the same bright shade as the sweater. "I didn't even realize I was still holding it. I'm so sorry." She practically threw it at him as she said, "I'm not going to take it after all, thanks." She grabbed Max's hand and pulled him out the door so fast, his feet barely touched the ground.

Once outside, Max doubled over, he was laughing so hard.

"That wasn't funny," Ava said, swatting him with her purse. She had a hard time holding back her own laughter.

He straightened up, trying to catch his breath before bringing his hand up to his ear, pretending to talk on the phone, *"Mom, it's me, Ava. I've been arrested for shoplifting ... and indecent exposure."* He took a few steps back as he started laughing again.

She put her hands on her hips, leaning her body toward him—with attitude. "Should I make that call before or after I tell my Dad about my new boyfriend, the nude model? I hear Santa's bringing him a shotgun for Christmas."

"Are you trying to scare me away, Miss Haines? Because I'm not going anywhere." He took his hands in hers, all signs of laughter now gone from his face. He looked deep into her eyes. "I'm here for the long haul, and I will gladly tell your parents so." Her eyes locked into his, as he continued to speak. "I don't want this week to end, and I don't want to leave you. Ever."

"I don't want to talk about that," she said, feeling the sadness starting to overwhelm her. "We still have a few days together."

"We do," he agreed, a mischievous smile suddenly crossing his lips. "And I've got something kind of shocking planned for later."

"Shocking?" she asked, raising her eyebrows. "I think you should know before this goes any further, that I'm pretty conservative. I'm not into any of that weird stuff... you know... in the bedroom."

Max started laughing again. "That's unfortunate—but not what I'm talking about." He chuckled again. "Perhaps shocking was the wrong word. Surprising probably is more accurate. I'm going to make you dinner—from scratch—something other than spaghetti and eggs. I woke up in the middle of the night and started watching one of those cooking show. I think I've got this."

Ava raised her eyebrows once again. "No, you were right, that is shocking," she laughed. "And now I'm definitely afraid. So, what are you making?"

"I told you, it's a surprise. Come on, we'll go to the market together, but no peeking okay?"

"O-kay. Are you sure *you're* not trying to scare *me* away?" Ava elbowed him in the side playfully.

"No way," he said as they walked toward his car. "You need me. Prison gets awful lonely without any visitors."

"Max Wallis!" she exclaimed, swatting him one more time. "You're terrible."

He stopped walking to embrace her in a passionate kiss, picking up where they'd left off inside the store.

32

Back at Max's apartment, Ava flipped through the magazine she'd picked up at the market for the third time. There was an awful lot of clattering coming from the kitchen, but she'd been given strict instructions not to enter under any circumstances. She wondered at what point going in would be a forgivable offense... After all, he had saved her once. The least she could do was return the favor.

She tiptoed toward the doorway.

"Max?" she said, not overly soft, yet not loud either— She hoped she could walk in and say, '*Well I called out to you, but you didn't respond, so I thought you needed help,*' with sweet puppy dog eyes.

Instead she heard, "Don't come in! Everything's fine. I'm almost ready. Just go back to the couch and relax. I'll let you know when it's done."

Damn. She headed back to her assigned seat and picked the magazine up once again. She'd managed to get a good whiff of whatever he was cooking when she approached, and while she wasn't able to identify the odor, it wasn't entirely offensive. She supposed that was a good sign.

After a several more clanks and a few creatively strung together curse words, Max finally emerged from the kitchen. He looked like he'd been to battle. His hair was a mess, his clothes were rumpled, and apparently, whatever they were about to eat had red sauce. Either that or he had blood smeared across his chest. Since he wasn't screaming in pain, and appeared to still have all his fingers intact, she assumed it was sauce—at least she hoped that was the case.

"So," Ava began, "what's the word? Are we ready for dinner?"

Max cringed. "I ... um ... I—" He reached into his back pocket and pulled out a menu to the local pizza parlor. Handing it to her he said, "What would you like?"

She covered her mouth to stifle her giggles, but a few managed to escape despite her efforts. "I'm sorry," she apologized. "Thanks for trying. It smells ... good."

"It smells like skunk," he said, laughing. "Guess I should stick to spaghetti and eggs, huh?" He looked down at his shirt and shook his head. "I should go change before the delivery guy gets here and wonders if we're hiding a body."

"Can I at least help you clean the kitchen?" she asked.

"Sure," he said, "but enter at your own risk. It's a war zone in there."

"You make a mean mushroom pizza, Chef Max," Ava said, unable to resist teasing him as she took another bite of their Plan B dinner.

She sipped her wine, enjoying both the food and the company, unable to remember a time when she felt this relaxed. Exams were over, graduation was in sight, her job was secured, she was with the man of her dreams, and Thomas was in jail, hopefully for many years to come. She'd barely thought about him in days. She wasn't going to let the fact that he'd popped into her head now ruin her perfect evening.

"Yes, well, it takes years of practice. I've got ordering down to an art." He winked at her and raised his glass. "Here's to us," he said clinking her glass.

"And to our fabulous gourmet meal," she added. She took a drink and studied Max as he looked down at his plate. "So, you said you had trouble sleeping last night. Is everything okay?"

"Yes. I told you before, I'm a light sleeper."

"Well there's a difference between being a light sleeper and not sleeping at all. Are you worried about something?"

"No ... I mean, it's nothing."

"What is it? Please, tell me."

"It's probably no big deal, especially since you don't seem to remember. But, you've been talking in your sleep. Crying actually."

"Really?" Ava paused. Holly used to complain that she'd talked in her sleep when they were kids, but she hadn't done it in years—at least, not that she'd known about. She also couldn't think of any dreams she'd had lately that would cause her to cry. In fact, she couldn't recall dreaming at all the last few nights. "What did I say?"

Max sighed a long breath before he continued. "You were yelling no, and a couple of times, you called out Thomas' name. I try to wake you up, but sometimes you're in such a deep sleep, you confuse me for him." He pulled up his sleeve to reveal scratch marks on his arm.

"Oh my God! I did that to you? I'm so sorry!" She couldn't believe she'd been fighting Max in her sleep and didn't remember any of it. Just the thought of hurting this sweet man that she cared about so much made her heart ache. She started crying, softly at first, then sobbing outright as she thought of what a good person he was and how lucky she was to have him in her life.

He wrapped his arms around her and let her cry on his shoulder. "You know I'd never hurt you, right, Ava?" he asked, his tender kisses on her hair comforting her.

She nodded as the tears continued. She had so many emotions to get through and let out. Not just for the feelings she had for Max, but also for the pain she'd suffered at the hands of Thomas. Pain she had yet to fully face.

He moved back slightly and lifted her chin to meet her eyes. "I'll do whatever I need to do to make sure you're safe. You have my word."

33

"You sure you'll be okay?" Max asked, standing next to her as he watched her pack.

Ava pulled her suitcase off her bed. It landed with a thud as it tipped over. Max picked it up and set it on its wheels for her.

"No," she replied, trying to swallow the lump that was trying to lodge in her throat. "I don't want to leave you, but it's been over a week, and my family is getting on my case. I really do have to get home, and so do you. Aunt Sheila's waiting for you, remember."

Laughing, he grabbed her around the waist. "I can't wait to tell Aunt Sheila all about you. Maybe now she'll leave me alone!" He kissed her neck softly. "I'm going to miss you, you know."

"You better," she teased, stopping before her emotions got too out of control. "I'm going to miss you, too." She could feel the tears starting to form, and she blinked rapidly hoping to forestall them. This last week had been one of the best she'd ever experienced. She and Max had spent every minute together, *as a couple*, getting to know each other without the stresses of school or family *or anything*.

"Think of this as a trial run. We've got just under three weeks apart over the holidays. Then we'll have an entire week together again," he said. His tone was upbeat, but Ava knew him well enough by now to know that was only for her benefit.

"Until you move across the country." She wiped her tears away. "How long until your first break again?"

"March—that's not long at all. I'll fly back here to visit, and in May you'll come out for a week, like we planned. Oh, babe, please don't cry! You'll see, it'll go by fast. I promise."

She nodded and buried her head against his chest.

She took a deep breath. "Can we stop by the gallery before I head out?" she asked, looking up at him for support. She still wasn't sure she was ready, but she knew it was time.

He smiled down at her, squeezing her hand to let her know he'd be by her side the entire time. "Of course. Cynthia will be so happy to see you. You can drop me off at my apartment after that, on your way out of town. Come on, we should get going before it gets too late for you to leave. If you put off your trip another day, Holly and Tessa might drive here themselves and drag you back whether you're ready or not. In fact, I'm surprised they haven't already to be honest. How'd you hold them off this long anyway?"

Ava's lips curved into a mischievous grin. "Told them I had the flu."

He laughed and shook his head. "Well, that's one way to keep them away. You're a sneaky one."

"I know," she agreed with a smirk. "I just ... I wanted to tell them about you—about us—in person. They're going to be mad ... and then happy. But first they're going to be really, really mad."

Letting out a low whistle Max said, "Glad I won't be there for that conversation. Yeah, um, good luck with that. And here I thought you didn't want to go home because you couldn't bear to be away from me. The truth is, you don't want to go home because you're terrified of your sisters."

Ava giggled, tracing the lines of his neck at the collar of his shirt. "Oh, you know you're the reason I'm not in a rush to get home. At least you're ninety-eight percent of the reason. Do you like how I threw in some statistics there?" She winked, trying to pull off a flippant attitude, but knew she'd failed when another tear slid down her face. "We should get going, though. The flu only lasts so long."

"Ava, dear! It's so good to see you!" Cynthia gave her intern a hug as she walked through the door, and then proceeded to kiss her on both cheeks in perfect Cynthia fashion.

"You got a bell," she noted, as the door closed behind them with a soft jingle.

"Yes, well, you know, I'm here by myself so much. If I'm in my office, I can't hear when someone comes in, so I thought ... well, of course, you were the one who came up with the brilliant idea."

"You remember Max?" Ava asked. "From the night of the exhibit?" She cleared her throat. She'd hoped the subject wouldn't come up.

"Yes, yes, of course! And we've spoken on the phone." She kissed both of his cheeks, too.

"The gallery looks wonderful."

She barely recognized the place. All traces of Thomas were gone. Usually when an exhibit ended, Cynthia kept one or two pieces on display, but none of his photos were around. She also had a wall where she displayed photos and news clippings of herself with the artists who'd been featured there in the past—sort of a *wall of fame*. Photos, or any mention of Thomas' affiliation with the gallery for that matter, were noticeably absent.

"I've had contractors in just about every day," Cynthia began. "I've been wanting to do some renovating for a while now. Well, there never seemed to be a good time since we've been booked with back-to-back shows. However, now that I had this week free, I decided to go for it."

Ava twirled around, trying to take in all of the changes. "The lighting is different, and the walls…" She walked over to where the office used to be, and noticed that the space had been completely opened up.

"Yes," Cynthia explained. "I decided to change the atmosphere in here. I hated having all of those museum-like enclosed rooms. So I had my crew knock them all down. Instead of walls, I've got these dividers, see? Partial walls that leave just enough room at the tops and sides to keep the open flow. What do you think?"

"Brilliant—I love it. Especially these curved walls in the center."

"Ava," Max said, rubbing his hand down the curvature of the wall, "you know what these remind me of?"

She smiled. Of course she knew. She'd seen the pictures so many times they were etched in her memory forever. It was the first thing that came to her mind as well. "The Musée de l'Orangerie."

Cynthia clapped her hands together in joy. "Ah, my protégé! I'm so proud you made the connection! But

Max? I didn't know you were an art aficionado as well."

He shrugged. "I wouldn't say aficionado."

Ava nudged Max and smiled. "Stop being so modest." She looked at Cynthia. "Max has been to the finest art museums all around the world."

"Is that right? And you didn't apply for my internship?" She pouted. "I'm hurt."

"Hey!" Ava said. "Then I'd be out of a job. Anyway, I can't believe your contractors were able to get all this work done so fast."

"Oh, you know, I can be persuasive when need be."

"So where's your office?" She'd been dreading stepping foot into that room—the scene of her attack since the moment they'd arrived. Just the thought of it sent her heart racing on the drive over. But now, she felt like she was in a completely different building. The space that was previously the office was now part of the gallery. Nothing about this place was frightening at all.

"Oh, that's the best part!" Cynthia squealed, her eyes lighting up with excitement. "Come!" She grabbed her hand and led her behind one of the divider walls, with Max following along. The space was painted in rich, bright colors and was filled with art, just like the rest of the gallery, but in the center sat Cynthia's desk and filing cabinet. "Isn't it great? It's private, yet I feel like I'm still part of the gallery, not tucked away in some stodgy office where no one will see me."

"It's wonderful! I still can't believe you pulled all of this off in just a week." As beautiful as it all was, she knew it was brought on by the attack, and she didn't blame Cynthia. She had to have been shaken up by the incident as well, especially since it involved someone she considered a friend. It had to be difficult for her to come to work every day, sitting here alone, pondering the events of that night. All of the changes she made to the gallery made perfect sense.

Cynthia put her arm around Ava's waist. "It just felt like it needed to be done," she said softly, then smiled again. "Onward and upward, right?" She patted Ava on the arm before grabbing her and Max by the hand.

"Now tell me, what's going on here between the two of you?"

They both broke into wide smiles as they filled Cynthia in on *almost* all of the events of the past week.

34

Ava sat in her car, driving along route ninety and trying her best not to think about the fact that thirty minutes had passed since she'd left Max at his apartment. Thirty minutes since she last saw him, last kissed him, even made love with him one final time. The next time she would feel his body and his lips close to her would be in three weeks. It seemed like an eternity. If she thought about it too much, she knew her vision would be clouded with tears, and she needed to concentrate on the drive. Only an hour and a half more until she'd be home. She wondered if Max had already left on his four-hour journey home.

It was the first time she'd been alone in over a week, and she had to admit that it was making her nervous. Just the thought of needing to make a stop at the rest area and walking by herself in the crowded building, without anyone to protect her, was freaking her out a bit. Logically, she knew Thomas was locked up miles away, but still, she'd rather keep moving. Getting home quicker to her family, her sisters in particular, was her only goal now. Thankfully, the freeway traffic moved swiftly and helped to keep her distracted.

Tessa was the first one to come running out of the house as Ava's car rumbled down the gravel driveway. She stopped short in order to avoid hitting her baby sister.

"You made it! You made it!" Tessa shrieked, nearly knocking Ava over as she tried to get out of the car.

Her mother came running out of the house, yelling, "Tessa! Give your sister some room to breathe. For God's sake, she's not well, and right before Christmas, too, poor thing!" She pulled her youngest daughter away and gave Ava a loving but brief hug before putting the back of her hand to her forehead. "How are you feeling, sweetie, are you doing better? You look a bit flushed."

Ava felt confused. Was she talking about the attack? And if so, how had she found out about it? Holly said their parents had, thankfully, missed the initial round of news reports, and as far as she knew, had no idea. She'd made Holly promise not to tell, so it couldn't be that.

Her mom continued, tugging her up the steps, "Come inside! It's too cold for you to be standing out here. I've got a pot of my homemade chicken soup on the stove. It's the perfect medicine for your flu."

The flu! Right! Ava coughed twice before saying, "Thanks, Mom, I do love your soup. I'm sure it's exactly what I need." She looked around, wondering why her other sister hadn't come out to greet her. "Where's Holly?"

"She'll be here soon. She and your father went to go pick out the tree at Asher's Farm. Dad figured you wouldn't be feeling up to it, and Tessa wanted to stay to see you more than she wanted to traipse around in the snow. Come on now, it's freezing out here. Let's go, we'll get your things inside when he gets back."

The chaos and confusion aside, there was only one thought running through Ava's mind ... it was good to be home.

"All right, Av," Holly said, "spill it. We know you don't have the flu. So why did you stay at school so long?"

The two sisters had cornered Ava as she was coming out of the kitchen with a plate of the lasagna their mom had made for dinner. Poor Ava had only been offered soup because of her *unfortunate* illness, and her stomach had been growling all night. After dinner, her parents and sisters decorated the tree while she watched from the couch.

Wrapped snugly in a blanket and sipping a cup of mint tea, she did her best to instruct them on the best places to hang the ornaments. Soft Christmas music played in the background, and a light snow was falling outside, and as far as she was concerned, it was a perfect first evening home. Almost perfect...

When the decorations were finished, Ava was sent straight to bed. She hadn't been able to call Max—she hadn't wanted her sisters or her parents to hear her talking—but she'd been able to answer his texts:

Max: Hey, babe. I miss you already. What are you doing?

Ava: Pretending to be asleep. My parents sent me to bed early because I'm "sick". Next time don't let me come up with an illness as an excuse.

Max: Oh no—can't you say you've had a miraculous recovery or something? Could happen, right?

Ava: I sure hope so, 'cause that's what I'm going with when I wake up tomorrow morning. How's it going there?

Max: Oh, you know. I already got the law school/med school speech. It wasn't too bad this time. My parents seem excited about flight school. Maybe they've had a change of heart.

Ava: And Aunt Sheila?

Max: Haha. She hasn't been by yet.

Ava: I wish I could be there to see her face when you tell her about me. I miss you. I miss having you next to me in bed even more.

Max: I was just thinking the same thing. When do you plan on having that talk with your sisters?

Ava: Tomorrow.

Max: Well, good luck. I'll talk to you then, okay? I'm going to turn in. That drive took a lot out of me. *xoxo*

Ava: Good night. xoxo

She stared at her phone, wishing she could make Max appear. Texts were nice, but they were a poor substitute for having him in the same room with her. Time away from him was going to seem like an eternity and lying in bed with her stomach growling didn't help.

Once she heard her parent's bedroom door close, she crept out of her room, down the stairs, and into the kitchen to snatch a piece of lasagna; she didn't care if it was cold. She was starving. That's when Holly and Tessa cornered her. She tried to fake a cough, but just giggled instead.

"Follow me," she whispered, plate in hand.

With practiced ease, the girls tiptoed back up the stairs and into the room Ava and Holly shared for as long as she could remember. Tessa, being six years younger, had always had her own room, while the two older sisters always roomed together. Now with Ava "sick," their mom had decided to move Holly into Tessa's room. *"No sense in all three of my girls getting sick for Christmas."* It seemed odd to have the room to herself, but when they climbed up onto Ava's bed, it felt like old times.

"So?" Holly asked, waiting impatiently for an answer.

Ava shoved a forkful of lasagna into her mouth. "Mom's lasagna is so good."

"Ava! Come on! Don't keep us in the dark," Tessa said, adding her orders to the mix. "We know you're hiding something. Tell us right now, or I'm going to scream. You don't want Mom to come running in here to see you eating that, do you?"

"Okay, fine," she said, finally giving in. She couldn't hide the huge smile spreading across her face any longer. "So I didn't have the flu."

"We already knew that," Holly said. "Keep going."

"And I wasn't with a friend all week after Thomas—" She paused, not knowing if Tessa knew about the attack. She hoped not. Sometimes she forgot that her baby sister was only sixteen. She was too young for parts of this conversation, so she'd have to give the censored version.

"After Thomas what?" Tessa asked. "He's that rich photographer dude who liked you, right?"

"Sort of. Well, we kind of broke up, and he had to go to … he had to go away. The whole thing was just a bad situation," Ava told her while keeping her eyes on Holly. "Anyway, I was pretty upset, so I told Holly that a friend was staying with me, but that wasn't entirely true. I mean, it was, but not in the way you think."

"Now I'm confused," Holly said, shaking her head. "So a friend, who isn't a friend, but sort of is a friend, stayed with you?"

"No. Yes. I mean ... well, he's more than a friend."

"He?" her two sisters asked together, raising their voices.

"Shh," she reminded them. The last thing she wanted was for her parents to come rushing in. "Yes, he." She smiled again and put her plate on the nightstand. "It was Max."

"You were shacked up with a boy this whole time?" Tessa asked with eyes wide.

Ava sighed. "It wasn't *shacking up*. We really care about each other." She looked over at her other sister. "You're being really quiet, Hol."

"No, it's good. I'm just ... this is the same guy who kissed you, then told you it was a mistake, then kissed you again, and *then* had a letter hand delivered to you to tell you that the second kiss was also a mistake. *That Max?*"

"It's not what you think."

She explained the circumstances surrounding the events leading up to the note and subsequent cold shoulder. The fact that he thought he was protecting her—how he really cared about her the entire time, how he honestly thought he was doing the right thing, how broken up he was about his decision. She tried to explain how nurturing Max was after she and Thomas *broke up*, but somehow it got lost in translation. She wished Tessa would give them five minutes alone so she could properly explain.

"So are you in love with him?" Tessa asked with her chin resting in her hands.

Ava smiled. "Well, we haven't actually gotten to the point of saying it yet, but … well …" Her smile grew even larger. "Yes, I do believe we are in love. At least I am."

Holly just continued to stare, while Tessa squealed in delight.

"Be happy for me, Hol."

"I am," she said, smiling and putting her arm around her sister's shoulder. "I really am. You've just had such a rough week. I want to make sure this is right. Long distance relationships aren't easy."

"I know, and to be honest, this first day has been really hard. But when I left home to go to college, leaving you two for the first time was really difficult, too. We'll just make it work, you know?"

Holly nodded and smiled. "It will get easier every day, you'll see. Just like it did for us." She kissed Ava on the cheek. "So you're in love, eh?"

She nodded and giggled, which caused Tessa and Holly to start giggling, too. "Shh," she reminded them again. "Mom and Dad are just down the hall."

Ava, Tessa, and Holly, snuggled together in the bed, until none of them could keep their eyes open any longer.

35

Ava could barely pull herself off the couch, and her mom worried that maybe she really did have the flu. In reality, she was suffering from a broken heart. Daily phone calls and frequent texting sessions just didn't seem to satisfy her growing need to be close to Max. What happened to the part about it getting easier every day? She began to wonder if maybe Max was right all along. Maybe starting a relationship when he was about to leave for the West Coast had been a mistake.

"Ava, it's Christmas, do you think maybe you could spend one day not moping around?" Holly asked, organizing the gifts they'd unwrapped earlier that day under the tree.

Holly always had to make piles; it was her thing. Ava guessed it was so she could compare which sister got the most loot, but their parents were always careful to make sure each of them received the same number of gifts. Her own stash included a new case for her phone from Tessa, a framed photo from Holly of the two of them taken at the beach over the summer, and a pile of new clothes from her parents, along with some assorted necessities for her apartment, including a cookbook. She'd let out a giggle when she opened it, thinking perhaps Max could borrow it. Max. She couldn't stop thinking about him.

"Yeah, Av! You're like totally killing my Christmas mojo here. You used to be the fun sister," Tessa stated, pouting from where she sat curled up. She'd spent much of the morning texting one friend or another.

"What?" Holly asked, turning to their youngest sister with her hands on her hips.

"Come on, Hol, you know what I mean. Ava's like our leader. She's the one who always comes up with all the cool plans and stuff. Like that time over the summer she helped sneak me into that bar so I could see my favorite band play. Remember that, Ava? Now that was fun." She slapped her hand over her mouth, her eyes wide when she realized what she'd said. "Oh shoot! You don't think Mom or Dad heard that, do you?"

Ava mustered an almost laugh. "No, they're upstairs, and I'm not moping. I'm just … I don't know … dreading."

"Well you're not allowed to dread on Christmas. Otherwise, I'll have to do something drastic." Holly motioned toward the piano.

"You wouldn't!"

"I would!" Holly smiled as she skipped over to the bench. "See," she told Tessa from across the room right before she started belting out Jingle Bells in the worst tone-deaf voice Ava had ever heard in her life, "I can be fun, too!"

"I'm not sure fun is the word I'd use," Tessa yelled, putting her hands over her ears.

"Ava, hurry up, the ball's about to drop!" Tessa yelled from downstairs.

She knew she should be down in the living room huddled around the television as she did every year to ring in the New Year with her sisters, but she couldn't pull herself away from Max. She longed to hear his voice, but didn't dare call him. She didn't want to hurt her sister's feelings. She just needed another few minutes to *talk* to him before going down to wish her family a Happy New Year. She typed:

Here's to a great New Year with lots of possibilities for you.

Max: For us, you mean.

Ava: Only one more week to get through until we're together again.

Max: I know. It's all I've been able to think about.

Ava: And then, you're leaving a week after that. I don't think I can handle it after all. This is so hard.

"Ava!" Holly shouted. "Come on!"

"I'm in the bathroom," she called back. "Not sure I'm going to make it in time to see it, but I'll be down in a few!"

Max: It is. But remember what you told me? If we believe in us, it will all work out. We will make it work.

Ava: Yes. It's just ... each day is so hard. I thought it was supposed to get easier with time, not harder. I don't think I can do this.

Max: Please, you have to try. For us. Babe, it will all be okay. Promise me you'll try.

Ava: Okay. I know. I will. I'm going to try ... I promise. It's a new year. New beginnings, right?

Max: Right.

Ava: Are you watching?

Max: Yeah, are you?

Ava: No. My family is, but ... I'm not with them. I'd rather ring in the New Year with you. I wish we were together.

Max: We are together – right there in Times Square celebrating. The streets are completely packed and all eyes are on the ball. It's completely encrusted in white crystals—the sparkle reminds me of your eyes with the light dancing through them. It's starting its descent now ... thirty seconds. I'm holding you tighter, waiting. Twenty seconds. I'm wetting my lips, getting ready. Ten – nine – eight – seven – six – five – four – three – two – one. I can see your smile in your eyes before you close them. I close mine as well and imagine our future together as I kiss you gently and whisper, "Happy New Year, babe. I love you."

Ava tried to wipe some of her tears away so she could see the screen on her phone. She typed back:

"I love you, too."

"Ava!" Holly pounded on the door. "You missed the whole thing! Are you okay? Come out. I'm worried about you."

She opened the door. Despite her efforts to wipe her eyes, she couldn't hide the swollen red rings around them.

"Oh, honey, don't cry," Holly said, pulling her sister in to hug her tight. "You'll be together soon."

"He loves me," she whispered.

36

"It's your turn, Ava," Tessa prodded.

They were playing Monopoly, normally Ava's favorite game. She was always so competitive when they played. She'd buy every property she landed on, including the utilities and railroads, and she'd never trade with anyone without squeezing out every last dime. Then, once she owned the monopoly, she'd build hotels so fast the other players wouldn't know what hit them. She had no mercy. You either paid up or were out of the game.

"*You sure you want to go into art?*" Dad always used to joke. "*You'd make a great slumlord.*"

Ava took the dice in her hands and put them down without rolling. "I think I hear my phone. You play without me." She raced up the stairs, cursing herself for not keeping it in her pocket like she normally did. She answered so quickly that she didn't have time to notice who was calling.

"Hello?"

"Remember me, sweetheart?" the British accent asked.

Ava's heart raced as she pulled the phone away from her ear and looked at the caller ID. *Private Number.*

"Where are you?" she whispered, sinking down onto her bed. She knew she should just hang up, and yet she continued to listen.

"The better question is where are you?" he replied. "I was just by your apartment, but apparently you're not there."

"I thought you were in jail," she said. *Hang up, Ava! Hang up.*

"I was, and now I'm not. My clever lawyers found a loophole. So I'd thought I'd stop by your place for a little chat. I never did get to finish thanking you. Are you at your family's house in Forest Hills?" Ava hung up the phone. Her hands trembled so much she could barely dial Max's number.

"He called me," she blurted out as soon as he answered.

"Who?"

"Thomas!" Ava shrieked. "Said he was out of jail and back in Wolfenson! He went by my apartment to *finish thanking me*, but I wasn't there. Then he asked if I was here. He knows where I am, Max! What if he shows up here?"

"I'm on my way. I was just packing to head back to school a few days early anyway. I'll come to your house instead. In the meantime, call the police."

"But you're four hours away!"

"Three and half ... under three if I speed. Make that call, Ava. Now! I love you."

"I love you, too. Be careful." Still trembling, she walked out of the bedroom, barely making it to the top of the stairs without collapsing.

"Ava!" Holly yelled from the living room where they were still playing Monopoly. "Dad just scored Boardwalk. You'd better hurry. I think he's getting ready to trade with Tessa. Hey, are you okay?"

"No," Ava cried. With one hand on her phone and the other on the railing, she tried to make it down, but stumbled on the first step. Hurrying up the stairs to catch her, her father helped her down the rest of the way, then over to the couch.

"Max," her mom said, coming down the stairs. "I've got the guest bed made up for you. Are you sure I can't get you anything to drink?"

"No, thank you, Mrs. Haines," he replied, trying to work up a smile.

Ava was curled in Max's arm as they sat on the couch. Tessa sat next to them on the floor, while Holly and her dad sat on the opposite loveseat.

"Have I told you how nice it is to finally meet you? Although I'm sorry we're meeting like this." Patricia Haines sat in the rocker across the room, glancing at her husband. "I wish we had known earlier. We could have helped."

"I didn't know either," Tessa stated, sounding hurt.

"I'm sorry," Ava said. "We just didn't want anyone to worry. He had so many charges piled up against him, we thought it was an open and shut case."

"I apologize, too," Max added. "I probably should have insisted Ava call or something. It's like she said. At the time we thought it was over."

"What's done is done," Bob Haines said. Ava had known the moment she'd told her family what happened, that her father had felt helpless, that he wanted to hurt Thomas, that he wanted to make everything better for her. They all did. "The important thing is that the police in two towns are now on the case. We've already filled out the paperwork for the temporary restraining order, so if that monster comes within a hundred yards of you, he can be arrested."

She nodded, unable to speak. Just the thought of Thomas coming within a hundred yards of her made her feel sick to her stomach.

"Ava, honey, why don't you go upstairs and get some rest? You looked wiped out. Dinner won't be ready for another couple of hours."

"I don't want to leave Max," she replied. "I can rest here." She adjusted her body into a reclining position, leaning into the warmth of his body.

Her mom pulled the quilt off the back of the couch and spread it over her daughter. "Girls!" she snapped. "Come on, let's give them a little privacy now."

Tessa and Holly groaned and followed their mother out of the room. Her dad got up, too, but stopped to give Ava a kiss on her forehead before leaving.

"I'm so glad you're here," she cooed, taking Max's hand and bringing it to her lips.

"Hey," he said, holding her closer, "I called the admissions office at my flight school as I was driving over. I told them I had a family emergency, and they said I could hold off on starting until next year."

She sat up and stared at him. "Absolutely not!" she said firmly. "No way."

"But ... I thought you didn't want to be apart to begin with, and now this. I won't be able to concentrate on anything out there if I'm worried about you."

"And I would feel guilty everyday if you stayed behind because of me. I'll be fine, honest. I've got the restraining order, and well, maybe I'll get a dog or something. One with big teeth." She showed her teeth, giving her best imitation of a vicious dog.

She knew she'd rather have Max stay with her, but she would never forgive herself if he did. It's not like he'd be able to watch her twenty-four hours a day anyway. She'd figure out a way to manage. She could always move back on campus and get a roommate or two. Plus, there were campus police all over the place.

Max smiled. "We'll talk about it later. You really do look tired," he said, "and now that I think about it, I am a little thirsty. I'm going to take your mom up on that drink. You want anything?"

Ava shook her head.

He kissed her lips, and then her forehead, before stroking her hair tenderly. "Okay, try not to worry, babe." He kissed her again and headed toward the kitchen.

37

The ringing phone jolted Ava out of her sleep. She reached in the air for it, caught somewhere in between her dreams and being awake. When the sound stopped abruptly, she slowly became aware of her surroundings, first wondering why she was laying on the couch in her parent's living room, and then wondering why it was so dark. And then she remembered. *Max.* He'd been there in the house with her, holding her, comforting her, telling her to get some rest. Where had he gone? In fact, where was everyone else? *What time was it?*

Ava sat up, pushing the quilt aside, and swung her feet to the floor. She inhaled deeply, relishing the aroma that brought back so many memories of her childhood. *It must be close to dinnertime.* There was no mistaking the smell of her mom's pot roast. As she got to her feet, she reached out for the wall to steady herself and to help guide her out of the living room and into the hallway. A faint light shone through the edge of the kitchen door, and she could hear her father's hushed voice coming from inside.

"I see," he said. "Well, it's never good news to get, but it's definitely a relief. Yes, sir, you have a good night as well. Thank you for calling."

"So what did he say?" she heard her mom ask.

"What's going on?" Ava asked. All eyes turned to her as she walked into the room. Her father was just hanging up the phone.

"You're awake." Max stood up and offered his chair to her. She smiled as she sat down, still feeling groggy.

"How was your nap, sweetie?" her mom asked. "You slept for a long time. Over two hours."

She looked around the table. "I hope you weren't holding up dinner on my account. You should have woken me up."

"Don't be silly. I'm just heating leftovers. They can wait."

Max put his hands on Ava's shoulders and kissed the top of her head. "You obviously needed your rest. I came right back out to the living room after I'd gotten a drink, but you were already fast asleep. I didn't want to wake you. Your family was all hanging out in the kitchen, so I thought I'd get to know them while you were sleeping. We've been talking this entire time."

Ava cringed. "Oh," she said, looking up to Max. "Sorry."

There wasn't anything *wrong* with her family per se. It's just that this was *the first meeting of the boyfriend.* True, it wasn't the ideal situation. Normally, whenever one of her girls invited a boy over for the initial meeting/interrogation, Ava's mom made a big dinner, a minimum of three courses—after an extensive menu planning session. There was always too much stress, plenty of nervous laughter, and usually a few kicks under the dinner table. It all went smoothly as long as nobody broke the rule: under no circumstance were you to leave said boyfriend unattended with said family for more than three minutes.

Holly nudged her. "Now stop, you know we are all perfect hosts. Well, everyone except Tessa. She got bored after fifteen minutes and went over to her friend Emily's house."

"That sounds about right." She laughed, but stopped quickly when she noticed her father. He was still sitting at the end of the table with his head in his hands and hadn't said a word since she'd walked into the room. "Dad?" Ava asked. "Is everything okay?"

"That was Captain Andrews on the phone," he responded flatly, motioning to the receiver on the counter behind him.

"The police officer who was here earlier?" she asked. She felt Max's grip on her shoulders tighten.

He nodded. "He received a call tonight from the Wolfenson police department. They found Thomas."

"Oh thank heavens," her mother said.

Ava breathed a sigh of relief. "Did they arrest him?"

He shook his head and replied, "No ... they didn't."

"What?" she cried. "He's clearly dangerous. First he drugged and attacked me, and now he's stalking me. Surely those are criminal offenses. And what about all the other women? He raped them! Why didn't they arrest him?"

Ava looked at Max with tears in her eyes. She couldn't believe this was happening. That horrible man was allowed to go free, to wander around the same town as her? Did they really think a piece of paper signed by a judge would keep him away?

"Mr. Haines," Max said, "did Captain Andrews say why they didn't arrest him?"

"Yes," her dad answered, looking first to Ava, and then around the table at everyone else. "Thomas is dead."

"*Dead?*" Ava whispered over the gasps coming from her mom and Holly.

He nodded, then explained, "They found his body this evening when the police delivered the restraining order. He was hanging by a bed sheet."

Ava turned and buried her head against Max's chest. As much as she hated Thomas, she didn't wish him dead. She only wanted him out of her life … preferably somewhere far away, where he could get help. Apparently he needed more than anyone realized.

"Captain Andrews said he left a note," he continued, his shoulders slumping.

She closed her eyes. The words would most likely haunt her forever. "What did it say?" she asked, hesitantly.

"Mostly there was a lot of stuff in there about how his career was over, and how he was nothing without that, which the detective said is pretty typical in these situations. It seemed like he'd really hit rock bottom. They found piles of his photos scattered all over his floor."

Ava nodded. "His career meant everything to him. Cynthia told me that with everything that happened, he'd been shunned in the art world. Every gallery that had offered to host him on his tour had cancelled, and his agent dropped him as well. I imagine it was a huge blow to his ego."

"You don't feel sorry for the guy, now, do you?" Holly asked.

"No, not really. I just never expected him to do something this drastic, but I guess it makes sense in a way." She thought back to the text Cynthia had sent her when she'd first gotten out of the hospital. She was right. He was so narcissistic that he couldn't handle anything less than having everything he felt entitled to—she supposed he'd rather check out than face his faults.

Her dad let out a long sigh before he finished with, "He also apologize to you and several other women, although it was mostly gibberish. That's pretty much it."

Ava pursed her lips and shut her eyes. Whether her father knew more and wasn't telling her, she didn't care. She didn't need to know his exact words. Max wrapped his arms around her, and she rested her head against him. The reality that she no longer had to worry about Thomas was starting to set in. She was ready to put this part of her life to rest.

38

Max followed Ava as they drove back to Wolfenson. He helped her unload her car, stayed for a short while, then left to go to his own apartment. He would be leaving for California in just one week and had plenty of packing to do. After they received the news about Thomas, Ava insisted he call the admissions office to his flight school to tell them he'd be starting on time. For the first time since the attack, Ava wasn't afraid to be alone in her own apartment, although she selfishly wanted to spend every minute of the week with Max.

She'd just unzipped her suitcase to begin the arduous task of putting her own things away, when she heard a knock at her door. *He couldn't stay away.* She laughed as she swung the door open.

"Ava!" Carly shrieked, throwing her arms around her friend and nearly knocking her over. "I've been sitting in my car across the street, waiting for Max to leave. I didn't want to walk in on you two … you know."

She pushed Carly away. "You've been stalking me?" she asked.

"Stalking's such an ugly word. I just missed you, that's all. Didn't you miss me, too?"

"Of course I did." Ava looked at her friend and smiled. They'd kept in touch regularly over break, but as with the case with her and Max, it just wasn't the same as having her around in person.

"Well, you sure seem a lot happier," Carly noted. "No offense, but most of your texts the last couple of weeks were downright depressing. To be honest, I was kind of worried about you. That's why I called Holly."

"You called Holly?" Ava asked, feeling both confused and a little annoyed.

"And Max," she said. "They didn't tell you?"

"No, they didn't. Why did you call them, and how did you get their numbers?"

Carly smiled and shrugged.

"See? You are a stalker!"

"Don't be mad. I just … you really sounded awful in your texts, like about to take a bottle of pills and wash it down with a bottle of booze awful. Usually, texts are

kind of like ... *hanging out with my family again.*
Grandpa ate too much chili, and now the whole room
smells like road kill ... blah – blah – blah. You know?"

Ava looked at Carly. *Honestly sometimes that girl*
comes up with the strangest stuff.

"I'm surprised neither of them told you I called,"
Carly said.

Ava rubbed her temples. "No, they didn't say a
word."

"Oh well, everyone was just concerned that's all.
They probably didn't want to upset you even more.
But now that Thomas is—" She stopped mid-sentence.

"It's okay, Carly. You can say the word dead. I
stopped feeling guilty over the fact that I'm relieved
about it days ago. Although the way he went was
pretty gruesome."

"If you asked me, he should have been strung up by
his—"

"Carly!" Ava snapped, shaking her head. "Stop.
Let's just move on. You were saying? Now that
Thomas is dead?"

"Well, I was just going to say that you can be a
little more relaxed now, and maybe you won't be so
bummed out all the time."

"Yeah," she said, going back over to her suitcase.
Sure. She continued to unpack. Why should she be
bummed out? The love of her life was across town,
preparing to move three thousand miles away in a
matter of days. Life was just grand.

"I mean, I know you're going to miss Max and all, but you still have me." she walked over to Ava and put an arm around her shoulder.

"Thanks." She knew Carly meant well, and she appreciated the effort. It wasn't her fault Max was leaving. It wasn't anyone's fault.

"Hey, did you get a chance to pick up your schedule yet?" Carly asked. "I thought maybe we could go into town together to get our art supplies for class and then stop at The Spot for some lunch. What do you say?"

Ava picked up her phone—no message from Max. He said he was going to text her when he was ready to get a bite to eat. As much as she wanted to see him, she really did need to get her schedule and supplies. Things tended to sell out quickly at the beginning of each semester. She quickly typed:

Hi. How's it going? What time do you want to meet for lunch?

Max: Hi babe. Didn't realize I had so much stuff. Can we make it dinner? Love you. xoxo

Ava: Sure. I'm going to grab a bite with Carly then, and I'll see you later. Love you back. xoxo

"Okay," she said. "That sounds like a plan."

"Cool. We'll take my car, you've been driving all day."

39

Ava looked at her class schedule as they sat at their table waiting to order at The Spot. For the first time in a long time, Statistics 101 wasn't listed. In fact, she only had one class left for her business degree—a marketing class. All the rest were art related. Graduation was in sight, as was a job with Cynthia. Everything she wanted was within her reach. Everything but Max. She'd have to wait longer for him. Why did there always have to be something? Why couldn't she just have it all for once?

The line at registration had been ridiculously long; not that Ava was surprised. Everybody returning from winter break had the same thing on their mind: getting their schedules so they could pick up their supplies to be ready for the first day of class. Of course, they would have gotten through a lot faster if Carly hadn't insisted she was thirsty, needing a drink that very minute. She'd made Ava leave the line with her to grab something at the student center just when they were starting to move closer to the front. She'd said if she didn't get some water that second she would surely pass out. Ava thought she was being a bit over dramatic, but whatever. Sometimes it was just easier to go along with Carly than argue with her. She'd noticed that Carly was checking her phone a lot as they got back in line—which was much longer than when they'd left it. Ava wondered if maybe she had a new boyfriend, although she didn't ask. She wasn't really in the mood for the details.

After they *finally* received their schedules, they headed over to the art supply store. As predicted, it was packed with students. She grabbed what she needed pretty quickly, but Carly seemed to be taking her time—texting someone all the while. Ava was starting to grow impatient. Just when she was about to suggest they skip lunch, Carly appeared ready to head to the cashier.

"Earth to Ava," Carly said.

"Huh?" she asked, looking up to see the waitress staring at her.

"Lunch, remember?" She motioned to the waiting server.

"Oh, sorry. I'll have a cheeseburger and a diet cola. Thanks."

The waitress scribbled the order on her pad and walked away.

"What's up? Did you forget to get something at the art store?"

"No, no. I'm sure I got everything. I was just thinking that for once, my schedule looks decent."

Carly took the paper out of Ava's hands and glanced at it. "Yeah, you look like a real art student, finally," she teased. "I'll bet Cynthia will be excited." She checked her phone again and smiled. "Hey, we should stop by the gallery when we're done so you can show her."

"Actually, I really just want to get back. I can tell her about it on Friday when I go in for work."

The waitress brought over the food and drinks, and the girls thanked her.

Carly took a long sip of her drink. "Oh, hey, speaking of the gallery, have you seen it? Cynthia had the whole place redone. Honestly, Ava, we should really just swing by. It won't take a minute. You'll love it."

"I already saw it," she responded, taking a bite of her burger. "Before I left to go home. You're right, it's pretty awesome. Why the sudden interest in stopping there?"

Her friend sighed. "Okay, well, I didn't want to tell you this, because it's supposed to be a surprise, but

Cynthia scored a big exhibit while you were gone. You know that painter Julien Henri?"

"Of course! He's amazing. We studied him last year in Art History. Are you saying Cynthia has his pieces in the gallery?"

Carly nodded.

"I thought most of his works were either in private collections or museums?"

"I don't know. You'll have to ask your boss. So, *now* do you want to stop by the studio? Or do you still want to wait until Friday?"

Ava looked down at her phone to check the time. It was getting late, and she really wanted to get home to Max. They could always stop by the gallery later that evening or tomorrow.

Carly took the last bite of her burger. "I'll tell you what," she said. "You think it over while I go use the restroom."

"Okay," she agreed. She glanced back down at her phone and started typing a message to Max:

Hey babe. Just finishing up lunch. Trying to get back to you ASAP so we can spend some time together.

She twirled her straw through her ice while waiting for his response. He seemed to be taking forever. Finally, her phone buzzed.

Sorry for the delay. Wasn't sure what time you'd be back with Carly, so my pal Ryan stopped by with a six-pack. We're going to watch the game for a little bit. Still on for dinner, though, right?

Ava: Sure. See you later.

Carly came out of the bathroom just as the waitress came by with the check. "So," she asked, "what's the story?"

"Oh why not," Ava replied, feeling annoyed. "We might as well stop at the gallery."

She stewed for the entire three-block walk. She and Max only had one week together—that's it—and they'd already spent most of day one apart. She understood that he needed to pack and all, but now he was just sitting around drinking beer and watching a game. Didn't he want to see her as much as she wanted to see him? Maybe he wasn't going to miss her after all. Just the thought made her even more upset. By the time they got to the gallery, she barely remembered why she was there.

"You've been so quiet," Carly said as they approached. "Everything okay?"

"I'm fine. Let's just go in." She hoped that seeing fine art would cheer her up.

Carly opened the door, allowing Ava to go in first.

She looked around the room, and then at her friend, who had the biggest grin on her face.

"What's going on?" she asked.

40

"Why are the lights off?" Ava asked Carly. "And where's Cynthia?" She glanced around the room, lit only by a small amount of hazy sunlight coming through the windows. "Cynthia?" she called out. "Something's not right here." She wasn't sure if she should stay and investigate, or leave and call 9-1-1. She just knew she felt extremely uncomfortable ... and Carly still had that goofy smile. She was definitely up to something.

"You made it, Ava," her boss said as she finally came out from behind one of the curved walls. "I've been waiting for you."

"Oh, there you are. Good." Her eyes were starting to adjust to the dimness as she spoke. "I was getting worried. What's with the lighting in here? I can barely see."

"I didn't want you to see my new exhibit until you were in the perfect spot," she said.

"Oh, you mean the Julien Henri exhibit?" Ava asked.

"Julien Henri?" Cynthia said while looking at Carly with a furrowed brow.

She just shrugged her shoulders and nodded.

"Sorry. I know you wanted to surprise me, but Carly already told me you have several of his pieces on display. You kind of picked the wrong person to tell your secret to. It's okay though—I'll still enjoy seeing them. So where are they?"

Cynthia sighed. "Fine, just follow me."

"I do appreciate the effort," Ava said, "I feel so special. You really didn't have to go through such a fuss. I would have been just as happy to come see the exhibit with all the common folk." She laughed. Through the dark, she swore she could see Carly roll her eyes.

"Oh well, I tried," Cynthia answered. "Now eyes closed until I tell you to open them." She put out her hand and led Ava into the biggest area of the gallery, the one where all of the curved walls gave the appearance of forming a circular space.

It felt like her boss was taking an extreme amount of time positioning her just so. Finally, after what seemed like forever, she declared, "Open your eyes!"

Ava gasped and spun around. The lights in the gallery were back on. Surrounding her on all sides were enormous canvas paintings of Claude Monet's *Water Lilies* mounted as panels to each circular wall just as they were in the pictures she'd seen of the Musée de l'Orangerie in Paris. With her hand on her chest, and her mouth hanging open, she proclaimed, "Oh, my! This is beautiful! The most beautiful thing I've ever seen."

"No," the familiar voice said, "you're the most beautiful thing I've ever seen."

She spun around again. Max stepped out from behind one of the curved walls.

"Max?" she asked, confused. "What are you doing here? I thought you were back at your apartment watching the game with Ryan."

"Now why would I want to waste my time doing that when I could be here with you?"

She smiled and took his hand in hers. "Can you believe what Cynthia's done here? Isn't it incredible?" she asked.

"Actually, this was all Max's idea." She walked to the center of the room with Carly.

Ava looked up at Max. "You did this?"

"Well, I may have mentioned to Cynthia that you always wanted to visit the Musée de l'Orangerie." His face beaming in delight over the success of his surprise. "I guess we came up with the idea together."

She twirled around one more time. "But how ..."

"Well, these aren't the originals, of course, but I called in a few favors to borrow these wall sized prints. It's my going away gift to you." Cynthia smiled.

"You're going away?" she asked, once again confused. If her boss left, what would become of the gallery?

"No, silly, you are!" Carly blurted out, clasping her hands together. "Oh, I just can't take this anymore. Max! Tell her!"

He took both of her hands and began to explain. "Ava, I know we talked about you staying here while I'm in California, but the thought of being separated from you was tearing me up inside. At first I just told myself to suck it up, you know? That lots of people have long distance relationships and do just fine."

She nodded, feeling the now familiar tears starting to form.

He continued, "But once we were separated for winter break, the reality hit as to just how difficult it would be. You seemed to feel the same way. Then I started getting calls from Carly and Holly. They were both telling me how sad you were. Miserable really. I was miserable, too. I didn't know what to do. I didn't know how we would get through with only seeing each other here and there." He tenderly brushed his thumb across Ava's face to catch the tears as they fell.

"I know, Max," she replied. "It's going to be so difficult. I don't know how—"

He put his fingers to her lips. "Ava, remember when I was at your house? In the kitchen with your family while you slept?"

She laughed. "I'm really sorry about that."

"No," he said. "They weren't giving me the third degree or anything. Okay, maybe a little bit." He leaned in and kissed her lips softly before continuing. "Mostly we were talking about you. Everyone was so worried about you. At the time we thought Thomas was still around, and your family was worried about what would happen after I left, so we started making plans."

"What kind of plans?"

He took a deep breath and let it out slowly. "Your parents did most of the work, but they decided it might be best if you moved out to California. They spoke to the admissions office at the college where I'll be finishing my academic semester. They offer a part-time program and have agreed to let you enroll in the five classes you need to graduate, although you'll have to be in class through the summer. Your mom even found an apartment for you, just blocks away from my place, but, I think that was just to make your dad feel better ... you know, so he didn't have to think about you staying with me. Didn't you noticed everyone sneaking around your back these last few days, on the phone, doing a lot of whispering?"

Ava just stared at Max without any movement or reaction. She could barely process what he was telling her.

Cynthia put her hand on Ava's shoulder and she turned to face her. "And I have a friend out there who runs a gallery. After I told her how fabulous you are, she agreed to hire you ... for a paid position. She's getting ready to retire and had been looking for someone to take over for her. She's willing to train you while you're in school, then after graduation, you'll be running the place."

Ava opened her mouth to speak, but didn't even know where to begin.

"It's all been arranged," Max said. "Of course, you don't have to go. You're still registered here if you want to st—"

"No!" she shouted. "Of course I want to go!" She threw her arms around Max's neck. "I just can't believe you all did this for me. Forgive me for the weird reaction, I'm just in a bit of shock, that's all." She turned to face Cynthia. "I don't even know where to start to thank you."

"I just made a phone call," she said, smiling. "Your merits speak for themselves. I am beyond sad to lose you, of course. I feel sorry for whoever comes to take your place. There's no way they can even begin to fill your shoes." She grasped Ava's shoulders and gave her a big hug. Before she let go, she whispered in her ear, "I love you, like you were my own daughter."

"Oh Cynthia, I love you, too," Ava whispered back, before walking over to Carly. "And you!"

"What?" she asked holding her hands out. "What did I do this time?"

"Oh, let me see," she began, laughing. "You called my sister and boyfriend because you were worried about me, you kept this a secret, *and* you just made me spend two hundred and fifty dollars in art supplies for classes you knew I wouldn't be taking."

"Hey, Max said to stall you. Who do you think I was texting all day? Besides, you could have said no. Anyway, take them with you. You can never have too many paint brushes."

"So I guess this means there's no Julien Henri exhibit?" Ava laughed.

"No, you nerd. Wasn't this enough?" Carly asked.

"Yes!" she hugged her. "Thank you, Carly. I'm going to miss you so much. You better come visit me."

"Are you kidding? I've already got my flight booked."

Ava went back over to Max. "Wait a minute," she said, looking at him, "you said my parents agreed to all of this because of Thomas. But now that Thomas is gone—"

"Now that Thomas is gone, they still agree it's a good idea. In fact, I think your mom is already making wedding plans," he replied.

"Wedding plans!" Her eyes opened wide. "Why would she be doing that?"

Max continued to gaze at Ava while he got down on one knee. "Ava, I know we're still getting to know each other, but I love you. More than I ever imagined I could love anyone. Every time I think about my future, you're in it, right by my side. It's not my future I'm looking at, it's our future. It's like you said a few weeks ago … the more we try to stay apart, the more we're pushed together. So let's stop being apart."

He pulled a small black velvet box out of his pocket and opened it. Inside was a beautiful diamond ring that Ava recognized immediately—her grandmother's ring. She gasped.

"Your father gave me this with his blessing. He told me the love he witnessed between us reminded him of his own love for your mother. Did you know that he proposed after their first date?"

She wiped away her tears and nodded. She did, but had forgotten all about it.

"I promise to love you always, and one day, I will fly you to Paris and anywhere else you want to go." He took a long deep breath and added, "Marry me, Ava."

Holly and Jared dropped Tessa off and headed over to Farrell's Pub, which was surprisingly crowded for a Sunday. Most of the tables were filled, and the band had already started. Country. Jared hated country music. He was a rock 'n' roll guy through and through. Holly spotted Ben and Michelle in a corner U-shaped booth toward the back of the room.

"Sorry it took us so long, traffic was horrible," Holly said, as she walked up to them.

Ben stood as they arrived, but Michelle stayed in her seat, sipping some sort of fancy bottled water.

"It's no problem," he said. "I hope you don't mind, we ordered drinks for ourselves already."

He signaled for the waitress to come back around as Jared slid into the booth on the other side of Michelle, leaving Holly to sit on the end, directly across from Ben.

"Michelle," Ben started, "I forgot to mention Holly also went to high school with us. Do you remember her?"

"Holly? Hmm … no, I don't think so," Michelle stated, her tone making it clear she must not have been important enough to remember. She turned toward Jared and smiled. "And I know you weren't there. I would have remembered you."

He shook his head, eyes glued to her. "No, I didn't grow up in Forest Hills."

"Too bad," she said, curling her lips back.

Holly reached for his hand.

"Anyway," Michelle continued, switching back to Holly. "I mostly hung out with upper classmen or college kids. I found most of the kids in our class to be … I don't know … ordinary."

Holly looked at Michelle and had to resist the urge to roll her eyes. She tried to shake it off.

Ben turned his head toward his girlfriend. "If I recall, you had plenty of *friends* in our class."

Holly opened her eyes wide. *Did that mean what she thought it meant?*

"Oh sweetie, I didn't mean it like that," Michelle cooed, running her hand seductively across his chest.

"You know I had a crush on you from the minute I saw you in English class."

Yeah right. You didn't even know he existed. You were too busy hooking up with the football team ... and the basketball team.

"We never actually dated in high school. Or even spoke, really—" Ben started to tell the Holly, taking Michelle's hand off his chest and placing it back in her lap.

"But, thankfully, we found each other this summer," Michelle said, finishing his sentence.

When the waitress came by, Holly and Jared each ordered a beer and Michelle ordered another bottle of imported mineral water.

"I don't drink alcohol," she explained.

"So, Jared, I heard you mention you wanted to come out tonight to celebrate?" Ben asked.

Smiling, Holly slid in closer to her boyfriend. "Jared was promoted today," she announced, leaning into him.

"Here, here!" Ben called, lifting his bottle up. "Congratulations. What kind of work do you do?"

"As of today, I'm a Team Leader for the maintenance crew at Crestmont Memorial Hospital."

"Maintenance crew. That's like, what, janitorial?" Michelle asked, wrinkling her nose in disdain.

"No," Jared said. That question used to bother him, but he'd been asked it so many times now, he automatically responded with his standard answer.

"I'm in operations. We work on special projects, plus make sure all the hospital equipment is up to code and functioning properly."

It may not have bothered him, but it bothered Holly. Not the question itself, but the way Michelle had asked it. Just because she was some high-powered executive didn't give her the right to peer down her snooty nose at everyone else. What did Ben see in her anyway?

"Can't have a hospital with shoddy equipment, that's for sure," Ben stated. "They're lucky to have you leading their team."

"I'm not leading the *entire* team," Jared explained. "Right now, I'll have a group of about ten workers reporting to me."

"One day you might be," Holly told him, snuggling against his side.

"I see. Well, that does indeed sound like something to celebrate," Michelle said, losing a bit of her condescending tone. Twirling her hair again, she shifted her body a little closer to Jared's.

Karen Pokras writes adult contemporary and middle grade fiction under the names Karen Pokras and Karen Pokras Toz. Her books have won several awards including two Readers' Favorite Book Awards, the Grand Prize in the Purple Dragonfly Book Awards, as well as placing first for two Global E-Book Awards for Pre-Teen Literature. A native of Connecticut, Karen now lives outside of Philadelphia with her family. For more information, visit www.karenpokras.com and www.karentoz.com

Thank you to my family and friends for your love, patience, and support. I feel so blessed to have you all in my life. A special note of gratitude to my beta readers, editor, cover designer, and cover models: Alicia Marietta, Tami Lee, Jane Anne Linsdell, Kathie Juliano, Kristy K. James, Melissa Ringsted, Najla Qamber, Courtney Boyett, and Willis Totten. Without your passion, creativity, critical eye, and attention to detail, Ava's Wishes would still be an idea swirling in my brain. Thank you for helping to bring Ava's Wishes to life. And to Author A.B. Shepherd — without you, my series would be nameless. You rock!

And to my readers—As always, thank you for believing in me and for your overwhelming support. Feel free to drop me a line - **I love hearing from you!**

karenpokrasauthor@gmail.com

Whispered Wishes Series:
Book 1: Ava's Wishes
Book 2: Holly's Wishes
Book 3: Tessa's Wishes
Book 4: Woven Wishes
Merry Wishes: A Whispered Wishes Novella

Chasing Invisible (Karen Pokras Toz)

Books for Children 7-12 (Karen Pokras Toz)
Nate Rocks the World
Nate Rocks the Boat
Nate Rocks the School
Nate Rocks the City
Millicent Marie Is Not My Name
Pie and Other Brilliant Ideas

www.ingramcontent.com/pod-product-compliance
Lightning Source LLC
Chambersburg PA
CBHW071143170626
46809CB00002B/745